RESURGAM !!

THIS BOOK BELONGS TO

Jennifer Louise Greig

THE COMPLETE TALES OF BEATRIX POTTER

"' . . . tippets for mice and ribbons for mobs! for mice!'
said the Tailor of Gloucester." *The Tailor of Gloucester*

THE COMPLETE TALES OF BEATRIX POTTER

The 23 Original Peter Rabbit Books

THE ORIGINAL AND AUTHORIZED EDITION BY

BEATRIX POTTER ™

New colour reproductions

F. WARNE & CO

*The reproductions in this book have been made using
the most modern electronic scanning methods from entirely
new transparencies of Beatrix Potter's original watercolours.
They enable Beatrix Potter's skill as an artist to be appreciated as never before,
not even during her own lifetime.*

FREDERICK WARNE

Published by the Penguin Group
27 Wrights Lane, London W8 5TZ, England
Penguin Books USA Inc., 375 Hudson Street, New York, New York 10014, USA
Penguin Books Australia Ltd, Ringwood, Victoria, Australia
Penguin Books Canada Ltd, 2801 John Street, Markham, Ontario, Canada L3R 1B4
Penguin Books (NZ) Ltd, 182–190 Wairau Road, Auckland 10, New Zealand

Penguin Books Ltd, Registered Offices: Harmondsworth, Middlesex, England

First published in this format 1989
5 7 9 10 8 6

Designed by Bet Ayer

ISBN 0 7232 3618 6

Printed and bound in Great Britain by William Clowes Limited,
Beccles and London

CONTENTS

ABOUT BEATRIX POTTER

Beatrix Potter at her farm, Hill Top, c. 1907

Beatrix Potter was born in 1866 and grew up living the conventionally sheltered life of a Victorian girl in a well-to-do household. She didn't go to school but was educated at home in London by governesses, and so had few opportunities to mix with other children. Her only brother, Bertram, was six years younger, and when he was away at school Beatrix's constant companions were the pet animals she kept in the school-room. She would watch them for hours, studying their behaviour and sketching them with great skill. Each summer Beatrix Potter's father leased a country house for three months, at first in Scotland and later in the Lake District. On these extended holidays Beatrix and Bertram were able to explore the countryside and learn about plants and animals from their own observation.

Beatrix Potter's career as a children's storyteller and artist began when *The Tale of Peter Rabbit* was published by Frederick Warne in 1902. Several firms had previously rejected the story, but the public loved it as soon as it appeared. Beatrix was bursting with ideas, and produced on average two books every year until 1910. The money she earned gave her some independence, although she was still living at home with her mother and father. In 1905 Beatrix's editor, Norman Warne, proposed marriage. In spite of opposition from her parents (who considered him "trade" and therefore beneath them), Beatrix accepted, but his early death from pernicious anaemia only a few weeks later tragically ended the engagement. The same year, she bought her first property in the Lake District, Hill Top farm in the village of Sawrey. After Norman Warne's death she spent as much time as she could there. The farm and surrounding countryside began to appear in her stories, and some of her best-loved illustrations show Lakeland scenes that have remained unchanged to this day.

In 1913, at the age of forty-seven, Beatrix married William Heelis, a local solicitor, and made Sawrey her permanent home. Writing and painting began to take second place to farming, sheep-breeding and buying stretches of the beautiful Lakeland countryside to ensure their conservation. For the last thirty years of her life, farming and the preservation of land were to become her main concerns and when she died in 1943 she left over 4,000 acres of land and fifteen farms to the nation. She was a remarkable woman, with a truly original imagination, artistic and literary talent, vision, and the strength of mind to find creative fulfilment.

THE TALE OF
PETER RABBIT

1902

ABOUT THIS BOOK

The story of naughty Peter Rabbit in Mr. McGregor's garden first appeared in a picture letter Beatrix Potter wrote to Noel Moore, the young son of her former governess, in 1893. Encouraged by her success in having some greetings card designs published, Beatrix remembered the letter seven years later, and expanded it into a little picture book, with black-and-white illustrations. It was rejected by several publishers, so Beatrix had it printed herself, to give to family and friends.

About this time, Frederick Warne agreed to publish the tale if the author would supply colour pictures, and the book finally appeared in 1902, priced at one shilling (5p). It was an instant success, and has remained so ever since. A pacy story with an engaging hero, an exciting chase and a happy ending, matched with exquisite illustrations, adds up to a children's classic whose appeal is ageless.

ONCE upon a time there
were four little Rabbits,
and their names were—

           Flopsy,

       Mopsy,

    Cotton-tail,

and Peter.

They lived with their
Mother in a sand-bank,
underneath the root of
a very big fir-tree.

    "Now, my dears,"
said old Mrs. Rabbit
one morning, "you

may go into the fields or down the lane, but don't
go into Mr. McGregor's garden: your Father
had an accident there; he was put in
a pie by Mrs. McGregor.

"Now run along, and don't
get into mischief. I am going
out."

Then old Mrs. Rabbit took a basket and her umbrella, and went through the wood to the baker's. She bought a loaf of brown bread and five currant buns.

Flopsy, Mopsy, and Cotton-tail, who were good little bunnies, went down the lane to gather blackberries.

But Peter, who was very naughty, ran straight away to Mr. McGregor's garden, and squeezed under the gate!

First he ate some lettuces and some French beans; and then he ate some radishes.

And then, feeling rather sick, he went to look for some parsley.

But round the end of a cucumber frame, whom should he meet but Mr. McGregor!

Mr. McGregor was on his hands and knees planting out young cabbages, but he jumped up and ran after Peter, waving a rake and calling out, "Stop thief!"

Peter was most dreadfully frightened; he rushed all over the garden, for he had forgotten the way back to the gate.

He lost one of his shoes among the cabbages, and the other shoe amongst the potatoes.

After losing them, he ran on four legs and went faster, so that I think he might have got away altogether if he had not unfortunately run into a gooseberry net, and got caught by the large buttons on his jacket.

It was a blue jacket with brass buttons, quite new.

Peter gave himself up for lost, and shed big tears; but his sobs were overheard by some friendly sparrows, who flew to him in great excitement, and implored him to exert himself.

Mr. McGregor came up with a sieve, which he intended to pop upon the top of Peter; but Peter wriggled out just in time, leaving his jacket behind him.

And rushed into the tool-shed, and jumped into a can. It would have been a beautiful thing to hide in, if it had not had so much water in it.

Mr. McGregor was quite sure that Peter was somewhere in the tool-shed, perhaps hidden underneath a flower-pot. He began to turn them over carefully, looking under each.

Presently Peter sneezed— "Kertyschoo!" Mr. McGregor was after him in no time.

And tried to put his foot upon Peter, who jumped out of a window, upsetting three plants. The window was too small for Mr. McGregor, and he was tired of running after Peter. He went back to his work.

Peter sat down to rest; he was out of breath and trembling with fright, and he had not the least idea which way to go.

Also he was very damp with sitting in that can.

After a time he began to wander about, going lippity—lippity—not very fast, and looking all round.

He found a door in a wall; but it was locked, and there was no room for a fat little rabbit to squeeze underneath.

An old mouse was running in and out over the stone door-step, carrying peas and beans to her family in the wood. Peter asked her the way to the gate, but she had such a large pea in her mouth that she could not answer. She only shook her head at him. Peter began to cry.

Then he tried to find his way straight across the garden, but he became more and more puzzled. Presently, he came to a pond where Mr. McGregor filled his water-cans. A white cat was staring at some gold-fish, she sat very, very still, but now and then the tip of her tail twitched as if it were alive. Peter thought it best to go away without speaking to her; he had heard about cats from his cousin, little Benjamin Bunny.

He went back towards the tool-shed, but suddenly, quite close to him, he heard the noise of a hoe —scr-r-ritch, scratch, scratch, scritch. Peter scuttered underneath the bushes. But presently, as nothing happened, he came out, and climbed upon a wheelbarrow and peeped over. The first thing he saw was Mr. McGregor hoeing onions. His back was turned towards Peter, and beyond him was the gate!

Peter got down very quietly off the wheelbarrow, and started running as fast as he could go, along a straight walk behind some black-currant bushes.

Mr. McGregor caught sight of him at the corner, but Peter did not care. He slipped underneath the gate, and was safe at last in the wood outside the garden.

Mr. McGregor hung up the little jacket and the shoes for a scarecrow to frighten the blackbirds.

Peter never stopped running or looked behind him till he got home to the big fir-tree.

He was so tired that he flopped down upon the nice soft sand on the floor of the rabbit-hole and shut his eyes. His mother was busy cooking; she wondered what he had done with his clothes. It was the second little jacket and pair of shoes that Peter had lost in a fortnight!

I am sorry to say that Peter was not very well during the evening.

His mother put him to bed, and made some camomile tea; and she gave a dose of it to Peter!

"One table-spoonful to be taken at bed-time."

But Flopsy, Mopsy, and Cotton-tail had bread and milk and black-berries for supper.

THE END

THE TALE OF
SQUIRREL NUTKIN

1903

About This Book

In 1901, Beatrix Potter was spending the summer with her family in Lingholm, a house on the shores of Derwentwater in the Lake District. She wrote a letter all about the squirrels she saw there to eight-year-old Norah Moore, daughter of her former governess: "An old lady who lives on the island says she thinks they come over the lake when her nuts are ripe; but I wonder how they can get across the water? Perhaps they make little rafts!" The letter then goes on to relate the story of Nutkin, the cheeky squirrel who is finally punished by Old Brown, an owl whom Beatrix has substituted for the old lady of her letter.

The finished book was dedicated to Norah. It contains many views of the beautiful lake, Derwentwater, largely unchanged today.

THIS is a Tale about a tail— a tail that belonged to a little red squirrel, and his name was Nutkin.

He had a brother called Twinkleberry, and a great many cousins: they lived in a wood at the edge of a lake.

In the middle of the lake there is an island covered with trees and nut bushes; and amongst those trees stands a hollow oak-tree, which is the house of an owl who is called Old Brown.

One autumn when the nuts were ripe, and the leaves on the hazel bushes were golden and green—Nutkin and Twinkleberry and all the other little squirrels came out of the wood, and down to the edge of the lake.

They made little rafts out of twigs, and they paddled away over the water to Owl Island to gather nuts.

Each squirrel had a little sack and a large oar, and spread out his tail for a sail.

They also took with them an offering of three fat mice as a present for Old Brown, and put them down upon his door-step.

Then Twinkleberry and the other little squirrels each made a low bow, and said politely—

"Old Mr. Brown, will you favour us with permission to gather nuts upon your island?"

But Nutkin was excessively impertinent in his manners. He bobbed up and down like a little red *cherry,* singing—

"Riddle me, riddle me, rot-tot-tote!
A little wee man, in a red red coat!
A staff in his hand, and a stone in
    his throat;
If you'll tell me this riddle, I'll
    give you a groat."

Now this riddle is as old as the hills; Mr. Brown paid no attention whatever to Nutkin.

He shut his eyes obstinately and went to sleep.

The squirrels filled their little sacks with nuts, and sailed away home in the evening.

But next morning they all came back again to Owl Island; and Twinkleberry and the others brought a fine fat mole, and laid it on the stone in front of Old Brown's doorway, and said—

"Mr. Brown, will you favour us with your gracious permission to gather some more nuts?"

But Nutkin, who had no respect, began to dance up and down, tickling old Mr. Brown with a *nettle* and singing—

"Old Mr. B! Riddle-me-ree!
Hitty Pitty within the wall,
Hitty Pitty without the wall;
If you touch Hitty Pitty,
Hitty Pitty will bite you!"

Mr. Brown woke up suddenly and carried the mole into his house.

He shut the door in Nutkin's face. Presently a little thread of blue *smoke* from a wood fire came up from the top of the tree, and Nutkin peeped through the key-hole and sang—

"A house full, a hole full!
    And you cannot gather a bowl-full!"

The squirrels searched for nuts all over the island and filled their little sacks. But Nutkin gathered oak-apples—yellow and scarlet—and sat upon a beech-stump playing marbles, and watching the door of old Mr. Brown.

On the third day the squirrels got up very early and went fishing; they caught seven fat minnows as a present for Old Brown.

They paddled over the lake and landed under a crooked chestnut tree on Owl Island.

Twinkleberry and six other little squirrels each carried a fat minnow; but Nutkin, who had no nice manners, brought no present at all. He ran in front, singing—

> "The man in the wilderness
>   said to me,
> 'How many strawberries grow
>   in the sea?'
> I answered him as I thought
>   good—
> 'As many red herrings as grow
>   in the wood.'"

But old Mr. Brown took no interest in riddles—not even when the answer was provided for him.

On the fourth day the squirrels brought a present of six fat beetles, which were as good as plums in *plum-pudding* for Old Brown. Each beetle was wrapped up carefully in a dock-leaf, fastened with a pine-needle pin.

But Nutkin sang as rudely as ever—

"Old Mr. B! Riddle-me-ree!
Flour of England, fruit of Spain,
Met together in a shower of rain;
Put in a bag tied round with a string,
If you'll tell me this riddle, I'll give you a ring!"

Which was ridiculous of Nutkin, because he had not got any ring to give to Old Brown. The other squirrels hunted up and down the nut bushes; but Nutkin gathered robin's pincushions off a briar bush, and stuck them full of pine-needle pins.

On the fifth day the squirrels brought a present of wild honey; it was so sweet and sticky that they licked their fingers as they put it down upon the stone. They had stolen it out of a bumble *bees'* nest on the tippitty top of the hill.

But Nutkin skipped up and down, singing—

"Hum-a-bum! buzz! buzz! Hum-a-bum buzz!
As I went over Tipple-tine
I met a flock of bonny swine;
Some yellow-nacked, some yellow-backed!
They were the very bonniest swine
That e'er went over Tipple-tine."

Old Mr. Brown turned up his eyes in disgust at the impertinence of Nutkin.

But he ate up the honey!

The squirrels filled their little sacks with nuts.

But Nutkin sat upon a big flat rock, and played ninepins with a crab apple and green fir-cones.

On the sixth day, which was Saturday, the squirrels came again for the last time; they brought a new-laid *egg* in a little rush basket as a last parting present for Old Brown.

But Nutkin ran in front laughing, and shouting—

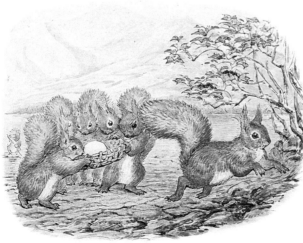

"Humpty Dumpty lies in
  the beck,
With a white counterpane
  round his neck,
Forty doctors and forty
  wrights,
Cannot put Humpty
  Dumpty to rights!"

Now old Mr. Brown took an interest in eggs; he opened one eye and shut it again. But still he did not speak.

Nutkin became more and more impertinent—

"Old Mr. B! Old Mr. B!
Hickamore, Hackamore,
   on the King's kitchen door;
All the King's horses,
   and all the King's men,
Couldn't drive Hickamore,
   Hackamore,
Off the King's kitchen door."

Nutkin danced up and down like a *sunbeam*; but still Old Brown said nothing at all.

Nutkin began again—

"Arthur O'Bower has broken his
    band,
He comes roaring up the land!
The King of Scots with all his
    power,
Cannot turn Arthur of the
    Bower!"

Nutkin made a whirring
noise to sound like the
wind, and he took a running
jump right onto the head of
Old Brown …!

Then all at once there was
a flutterment and a scuffle-
ment and a loud "Squeak!"

The other squirrels scuttered away into the bushes.

When they came back very
cautiously, peeping round the
tree—there was Old Brown
sitting on his door-step,
quite still, with his eyes
closed, as if nothing had
happened.

*   *   *   *   *

*But Nutkin was in his
waistcoat pocket!*

This looks like the end of the story; but it isn't.

Old Brown carried Nutkin into his house, and held him up by the tail, intending to skin him; but Nutkin pulled so very hard that his tail broke in two, and he dashed up the staircase and escaped out of the attic window.

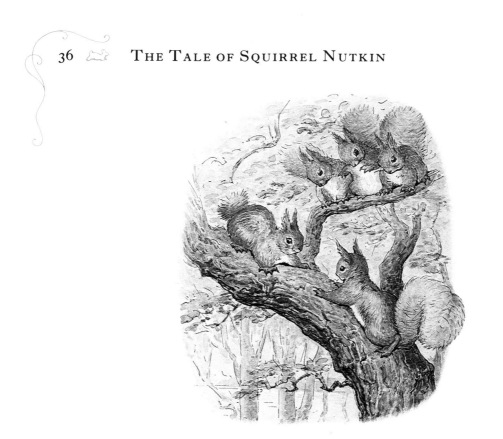

And to this day, if you meet Nutkin up a tree and ask him a riddle, he will throw sticks at you, and stamp his feet and scold, and shout—

"Cuck-cuck-cuck-cur-r-r-cuck-k-k!"

THE END

The Tailor of Gloucester

1903

"I'LL BE AT CHARGES FOR A LOOKING-GLASS;
AND ENTERTAIN A SCORE OR TWO OF TAILORS."
Richard III

ABOUT THIS BOOK

The Tailor of Gloucester was Beatrix Potter's own favourite among all her books. She first heard the true story on which it is based when visiting her cousin, Caroline Hutton, who lived near Gloucester. Leaving an unfinished waistcoat for the Mayor of Gloucester in his shop one Saturday morning, a tailor was amazed to find it ready on the Monday, except for one buttonhole, for which there was "no more twist". In reality, his two assistants had secretly completed the job, but Beatrix Potter has the work finished by little brown mice. She adds an extra note of enchantment by setting the story on Christmas Eve, when animals can talk, and weaving in many of her favourite traditional rhymes. The book was dedicated to another of the Moore children, this time to Freda, "because you are fond of fairy-tales, and have been ill."

IN the time of swords and periwigs and full-skirted coats with flowered lappets—when gentlemen wore ruffles, and gold-laced waistcoats of paduasoy and taffeta—there lived a tailor in Gloucester.

He sat in the window of a little shop in Westgate Street, cross-legged on a table, from morning till dark.

All day long while the light lasted he sewed and snippeted, piecing out his satin and pompadour, and lutestring; stuffs had strange names, and were very expensive in the days of the Tailor of Gloucester.

But although he sewed fine silk for his neighbours, he himself was very, very poor—a little old man in spectacles, with a pinched face, old crooked fingers, and a suit of thread-bare clothes.

He cut his coats without waste, according to his embroidered cloth; they were very small ends and snippets that lay about upon the table—"Too narrow breadths for nought—except waistcoats for mice," said the tailor.

One bitter cold day near Christmas-time the tailor began to make a coat—a coat of cherry-coloured corded silk embroidered with pansies and roses, and a cream-coloured satin waistcoat—trimmed with gauze and green worsted chenille—for the Mayor of Gloucester.

The tailor worked and worked, and he talked to himself. He measured the silk, and turned it round and round, and trimmed it into shape with his shears; the table was all littered with cherry-coloured snippets.

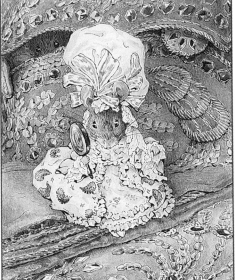

"No breadth at all, and cut on the cross; it is no breadth at all; tippets for mice and ribbons for mobs! for mice!" said the Tailor of Gloucester.

When the snow-flakes came down against the small leaded window-panes and shut out the light, the tailor had done his day's work; all the silk and satin lay cut out upon the table.

There were twelve pieces for the coat and four pieces for the waistcoat; and there were pocket flaps and cuffs, and buttons all

in order. For the lining of the coat there was fine yellow taffeta; and for the button-holes of the waist-coat, there was cherry-coloured twist. And everything was ready to sew together in the morning, all measured and sufficient—except that there was wanting just one single skein of cherry-coloured twisted silk.

The tailor came out of his shop at dark, for he did not sleep there at nights; he fastened the window

and locked the door, and took away the key. No one lived there at night but little brown mice, and they run in and out without any keys!

For behind the wooden wainscots of all the old houses in Gloucester, there are little mouse staircases and secret trap-doors; and the mice run from house to house through those long narrow passages; they can run all over the town without going into the streets.

But the tailor came out of his shop, and shuffled home through the snow. He lived quite near by in College Court, next the doorway to College Green; and although it was not a big house, the tailor was so poor he only rented the kitchen.

He lived alone with his cat; it was called Simpkin.

Now all day long while the tailor was out at work, Simpkin kept house by himself; and he also was fond of the mice, though he gave them no satin for coats!

"Miaw?" said the cat when the tailor opened the door. "Miaw?"

The tailor replied—"Simpkin, we shall make our fortune, but I am worn to a ravelling. Take this groat (which is our last fourpence) and Simpkin, take a china pipkin; buy a penn'orth of bread, a pen-

n'orth of milk and a penn'orth of sausages. And oh, Simpkin, with the last penny of our fourpence buy me one penn'orth of cherry-coloured silk. But do not lose the last penny of the fourpence, Simpkin, or I am undone and worn to a thread-paper, for I have NO MORE TWIST."

Then Simpkin again said, "Miaw?" and took the groat and the pipkin, and went out into the dark.

The tailor was very tired and beginning to be ill. He sat down by the hearth and talked to himself about that wonderful coat.

"I shall make my fortune—to be cut bias—the Mayor of Gloucester is to be married on Christmas Day in the morning, and he hath ordered a coat and an embroidered waistcoat—to be lined with yellow taffeta—and the taffeta sufficeth; there is no more left over in snippets than will serve to make tippets for mice—"

Then the tailor started; for suddenly, interrupting him, from the dresser at the other side of the kitchen came a number of little noises—

Tip tap, tip tap, tip tap tip!

"Now what can that be?" said the Tailor of Gloucester, jumping up from his chair. The dresser was covered with crockery and pipkins,

willow pattern plates, and tea-cups and mugs.

The tailor crossed the kitchen, and stood quite still beside the dresser, listening, and peering through his spectacles. Again from under a tea-cup, came those funny little noises—

Tip tap, tip tap, tip tap tip!

"This is very peculiar," said the Tailor of Gloucester; and he lifted up the tea-cup which was upside down. Out stepped a little live lady mouse, and made a curtsey to the tailor! Then she hopped away down off the dresser, and under the wainscot.

The tailor sat down again by the fire, warming his poor cold hands, and mumbling to himself—

"The waistcoat is cut out from peach-coloured satin—tambour stitch and rose-buds in beautiful floss silk. Was I wise to entrust my last fourpence to Simpkin? One-and-twenty button-holes of cherry-coloured twist!"

But all at once, from the dresser, there came other little noises:

Tip tap, tip tap, tip tap tip!

"This is passing extraordinary!" said the Tailor of Gloucester, and

turned over another tea-cup, which was upside down. Out stepped a little gentleman mouse, and made a bow to the tailor!

And then from all over the dresser came a chorus of little tappings, all sounding together, and answering one another, like watch-beetles in an old worm-eaten window-shutter—

Tip tap, tip tap, tip tap tip!

And out from under tea-cups and from under bowls and basins, stepped other and more little mice who hopped away down off the dresser and under the wainscot.

The tailor sat down, close over the fire, lamenting—"One-and-twenty button-holes of cherry-coloured silk! To be finished by noon of Saturday: and this is Tuesday evening. Was it right to let loose those mice, undoubtedly the property of Simpkin? Alack, I am undone, for I have no more twist!"

The little mice came out again, and listened to the tailor; they took notice of the pattern of that wonderful coat. They whispered to one another about the taffeta lining, and about little mouse tippets.

And then all at once they all ran away together down the passage behind the wainscot, squeaking and calling to one another, as they ran from house to house; and not one mouse was left in the tailor's kitchen when Simpkin came back with the pipkin of milk!

Simpkin opened the door and bounced in, with an angry "G-r-r-miaw!" like a cat that is vexed: for he hated the snow, and there was snow in his ears, and snow in his collar at the back of his neck. He put down the loaf and the sausages upon the dresser, and sniffed.

"Simpkin," said the tailor, "where is my twist?"

But Simpkin set down the pipkin of milk upon the dresser, and looked suspiciously at the tea-cups. He wanted his supper of little fat mouse!

"Simpkin," said the tailor, "where is my TWIST?"

But Simpkin hid a little parcel privately in the tea-pot, and spit and growled at the tailor; and if Simpkin had been able to talk, he would have asked: "Where is my MOUSE?"

"Alack, I am undone!" said the Tailor of Gloucester, and went sadly to bed.

All that night long Simpkin hunted and searched through the kitchen, peeping into cupboards and under the wainscot, and into the tea-pot where he had hidden that twist; but still he found never a mouse!

Whenever the tailor muttered and talked in his sleep, Simpkin said "Miaw-ger-r-w-s-s-ch!" and made strange horrid noises, as cats do at night.

For the poor old tailor was very ill with a fever, tossing and turning in his four-post bed; and still in his dreams he mumbled—"No more twist! No more twist!"

All that day he was ill, and the next day, and the next; and what should become of the cherry-coloured coat? In the tailor's shop in Westgate Street the embroidered silk and satin lay cut out upon the table—one-and-twenty button-holes—and who should come to sew them, when the window was barred, and the door was fast locked?

But that does not hinder the little brown mice; they run in and out without any keys through all the old houses in Gloucester!

Out of doors the market folks went trudging through the snow to buy their geese and turkeys, and to bake their Christmas pies; but there would be no Christmas dinner for Simpkin and the poor old Tailor of Gloucester.

The tailor lay ill for three days and nights; and then it was Christmas Eve, and very late at night. The moon climbed up over the roofs and chimneys, and looked down over the gateway into College Court. There were no lights in the windows, nor any sound in the houses; all the city of Gloucester was fast asleep under the snow.

And still Simpkin wanted his mice, and he mewed as he stood beside the four-post bed.

But it is in the old story that all the beasts can talk, in the night between Christmas Eve and Christmas Day in the morning (though there are very few folk that can hear them, or know what it is that they say).

When the Cathedral clock struck twelve there was an answer—like an echo of the chimes—and Simpkin heard it, and came out of the tailor's door, and wandered about in the snow.

From all the roofs and gables and old wooden houses in Gloucester came a thousand merry voices singing the old Christmas rhymes—all the old songs that ever I heard of, and some that I don't know, like Whittington's bells.

First and loudest the cocks cried out: "Dame, get up, and bake your pies!"

"Oh, dilly, dilly, dilly!" sighed Simpkin.

And now in a garret there were lights and sounds of dancing, and cats came from over the way.

"Hey, diddle, diddle, the cat and the fiddle! All the cats in Gloucester—except me," said Simpkin.

Under the wooden eaves the starlings and sparrows sang of Christmas pies; the jack-daws woke up in the Cathedral tower; and although it was the middle of the night the throstles and robins sang; the air was quite full of little twittering tunes.

But it was all rather provoking to poor hungry Simpkin!

Particularly he was vexed with some little shrill voices from behind a wooden lattice. I think that they

were bats, because they always have very small voices—especially in a black frost, when they talk in their sleep, like the Tailor of Gloucester.

They said something mysterious that sounded like—

"Buz, quoth the blue fly; hum, quoth
    the bee;
Buz and hum they cry, and so do we!"

and Simpkin went away shaking his ears as if he had a bee in his bonnet.

From the tailor's shop in West-gate came a glow of light; and when Simpkin crept up to peep in at the window it was full of candles. There was a snippeting of scissors, and snappeting of thread; and little mouse voices sang loudly and gaily—

"Four-and-twenty tailors
Went to catch a snail,
The best man amongst them
Durst not touch her tail;
She put out her horns
Like a little kyloe cow,
Run, tailors, run! or she'll have you all
    e'en now!"

Then without a pause the little mouse voices went on again—

"Sieve my lady's oatmeal,
Grind my lady's flour,
Put it in a chestnut,
Let it stand an hour—"

"Mew! Mew!" interrupted Simpkin, and he scratched at the door.

But the key was under the tailor's pillow, he could not get in.

The little mice only laughed, and tried another tune—

"Three little mice sat down to spin,
Pussy passed by and she peeped in.
What are you at, my fine little men?
Making coats for gentlemen.
Shall I come in and cut off your threads?
Oh, no, Miss Pussy, you'd bite off
    our heads!"

"Mew! Mew!" cried Simpkin.
"Hey diddle dinketty?"
answered the little mice—

"Hey diddle dinketty, poppetty pet!
The merchants of London they wear
    scarlet;
Silk in the collar, and gold in the hem,
So merrily march the merchantmen!"

They clicked their thimbles to mark the time, but none of the songs pleased Simpkin; he sniffed and mewed at the door of the shop.

"And then I bought
A pipkin and a popkin,
A slipkin and a slopkin,
All for one farthing—

—and upon the kitchen dresser!" added the rude little mice.

"Mew! scratch! scratch!" scuffled Simpkin on the window-sill; while the little mice inside sprang to their feet, and all began to shout at once in little twittering voices: "No more twist! No more twist!" And they barred up the window shutters and shut out Simpkin.

But still through the nicks in the shutters he could hear the click of thimbles, and little mouse voices singing—

"No more twist! No more twist!"

Simpkin came away from his shop and went home, considering in his mind. He found the poor old tailor without fever, sleeping peacefully.

Then Simpkin went on tip-toe and took a little parcel of silk out of the tea-pot, and looked at it in the moonlight; and he felt quite ashamed of his badness compared with those good little mice!

When the tailor awoke in the morning, the first thing which he saw upon the patchwork quilt, was a skein of cherry-coloured twisted silk, and beside his bed stood the repentant Simpkin!

"Alack, I am worn to a ravelling," said the Tailor of Gloucester, "but I have my twist!"

The sun was shining on the snow when the tailor got up and dressed, and came out into the street with Simpkin running before him.

The starlings whistled on the chimney stacks, and the throstles and robins sang—but they sang their own little noises, not the words they had sung in the night.

"Alack," said the tailor, "I have

my twist; but no more strength—
nor time—than will serve to make
me one single button-hole; for this
is Christmas Day in the Morning!
The Mayor of Gloucester shall be
married by noon—and where is
his cherry-coloured coat?"

He unlocked the door of the
little shop in Westgate Street, and
Simpkin ran in, like a cat that
expects something.

But there was no one there! Not
even one little brown mouse!

The boards were swept clean; the little ends of thread and the
little silk snippets were all tidied away, and gone from off the floor.

But upon the table—oh joy! the tailor gave a shout—there,
where he had left plain cuttings of silk—there lay the most
beautifullest coat and embroidered satin waistcoat that ever were
worn by a Mayor of Gloucester.

There were roses and pansies
upon the facings of the coat; and
the waistcoat was worked with
poppies and corn-flowers.

Everything was finished except
just one single cherry-coloured
button-hole, and where that button-
hole was wanting there was pinned
a scrap of paper with these words—
in little teeny weeny writing—

NO MORE TWIST

And from then began the luck of the Tailor of Gloucester; he grew quite stout, and he grew quite rich.

He made the most wonderful waistcoats for all the rich merchants of Gloucester, and for all the fine gentlemen of the country round.

Never were seen such ruffles, or such embroidered cuffs and lappets! But his button-holes were the greatest triumph of it all.

The stitches of those button-holes were so neat—*so* neat—I wonder how they could be stitched by an old man in spectacles, with crooked old fingers, and a tailor's thimble.

The stitches of those button-holes were so small—*so* small—they looked as if they had been made by little mice!

THE END

THE TALE OF
BENJAMIN BUNNY

1904

ABOUT THIS BOOK

The real-life Benjamin Bunny was a tame rabbit of Beatrix Potter's, whom she sketched constantly, and whose exploits continually amused her. "He is an abject coward, but believes in bluster, could stare our old dog out of countenance, chase a cat that has turned tail." Although Benjamin had died by 1904, when this story was published, Beatrix may well have been thinking of him when she created Peter Rabbit's cousin, Benjamin. Little Benjamin is a very self-possessed animal, who makes himself quite at home in Mr. McGregor's garden.

Beatrix sketched background scenes for the tale while on holiday in Fawe Park, a house with a beautiful garden in the Lake District. The book is dedicated to "the children of Sawrey from Old Mr. Bunny." Beatrix was later to settle in the Lake District village of Sawrey, buying a small farm there in 1905.

ONE morning a little
rabbit sat on a bank.
He pricked his ears and
listened to the trit-trot,
trit-trot of a pony.

A gig was coming along
the road; it was driven by
Mr. McGregor, and beside
him sat Mrs. McGregor in
her best bonnet.

As soon as they had
passed, little Benjamin
Bunny slid down into the
road, and set off—with a
hop, skip and a jump—to
call upon his relations, who
lived in the wood at the
back of Mr. McGregor's
garden.

That wood was full of rabbit holes; and in the neatest sandiest hole of all, lived Benjamin's aunt and his cousins—Flopsy, Mopsy, Cotton-tail and Peter.

Old Mrs. Rabbit was a widow; she earned her living by knitting rabbit-wool mittens and muffetees (I once bought a pair at a bazaar). She also sold herbs, and rosemary tea, and rabbit-tobacco (which is what *we* call lavender).

Little Benjamin did not very much want to see his Aunt.

He came round the back of the fir-tree, and nearly tumbled upon the top of his Cousin Peter.

Peter was sitting by himself. He looked poorly, and was dressed in a red cotton pocket-handkerchief.

"Peter,"—said little Benjamin, in a whisper—"who has got your clothes?"

Peter replied—"The scarecrow in Mr. McGregor's garden," and described how he had been chased about the garden, and had dropped his shoes and coat.

Little Benjamin sat down beside his cousin, and assured him that Mr. McGregor had gone out in a gig, and Mrs. McGregor also; and certainly for the day, because she was wearing her best bonnet.

Peter said he hoped that it would rain.

At this point, old Mrs. Rabbit's voice was heard inside the rabbit hole, calling— "Cotton-tail! Cotton-tail! Fetch some more camomile!"

Peter said he thought he might feel better if he went for a walk.

They went away hand in hand, and got upon the flat top of the wall at the bottom of the wood. From here they looked down into Mr. McGregor's garden. Peter's coat and shoes were plainly to be seen upon the scare-crow, topped with an old tam-o-shanter of Mr. McGregor's.

Little Benjamin said, "It spoils people's clothes to squeeze under a gate; the proper way to get in, is to climb down a pear tree."

Peter fell down head first; but it was of no consequence, as the bed below was newly raked and quite soft.

It had been sown with lettuces.

They left a great many odd little foot-marks all over the bed, especially little Benjamin, who was wearing clogs.

Little Benjamin said that the first thing to be done was to get back Peter's clothes, in order that they might be able to use the pocket-handkerchief.

They took them off the scarecrow. There had been rain during the night; there was water in the shoes, and the coat was somewhat shrunk.

Benjamin tried on the tam-o-shanter, but it was too big for him.

Then he suggested that they should fill the pocket-handkerchief with onions, as a little present for his Aunt.

Peter did not seem to be enjoying himself; he kept hearing noises.

Benjamin, on the contrary, was perfectly at home, and ate a lettuce leaf. He said that he was in the habit of coming to the garden with his father to get lettuces for their Sunday dinner.

(The name of little Benjamin's papa was old Mr. Benjamin Bunny.)

The lettuces certainly were very fine.

Peter did not eat anything; he said he should like to go home. Presently he dropped half the onions.

Little Benjamin said that it was not possible to get back up the pear-tree, with a load of vegetables. He led the way boldly towards the other end of the garden. They went along a little walk on planks, under a sunny red-brick wall.

The mice sat on their door-steps cracking cherry-stones, they winked at Peter Rabbit and little Benjamin Bunny.

Presently Peter let the pocket-handkerchief go again.

They got amongst flowerpots, and frames and tubs; Peter heard noises worse than ever, his eyes were as big as lolly-pops!

He was a step or two in front of his cousin, when he suddenly stopped.

This is what those little rabbits saw round that corner!

Little Benjamin took one look, and then, in half a minute less than no time, he hid himself and Peter and the onions underneath a large basket . . .

The cat got up and stretched herself, and came and sniffed at the basket.

Perhaps she liked the smell of onions!

Anyway, she sat down upon the top of the basket.

She sat there for *five hours*.

*   *   *

I cannot draw you a picture of Peter and Benjamin underneath the basket, because it was quite dark, and because the smell of onions was fearful; it made Peter Rabbit and little Benjamin cry.

The sun got round behind the wood, and it was quite late in the afternoon; but still the cat sat upon the basket.

At length there was a pitter-patter, pitter-patter, and some bits of mortar fell from the wall above.

The cat looked up and saw old Mr. Benjamin Bunny prancing along the top of the wall of the upper terrace.

He was smoking a pipe of rabbit-tobacco, and had a little switch in his hand.

He was looking for his son.

Old Mr. Bunny had no opinion whatever of cats.

He took a tremendous jump off the top of the wall on to the top of the cat, and cuffed it off the basket, and kicked it into the green-house, scratching off a handful of fur. The cat was too much surprised to scratch back.

When old Mr. Bunny had driven the cat into the green-house, he locked the door.

Then he came back to the basket and took out his son Benjamin by the ears, and whipped him with the little switch.

Then he took out his nephew Peter.

Then he took out the handkerchief of onions, and marched out of the garden.

When Mr. McGregor returned about half an hour later, he observed several things which perplexed him.

It looked as though some person had been walking all over the garden in a pair of clogs—only the foot-marks were too ridiculously little!

Also he could not under-stand how the cat could have managed to shut herself up *inside* the green-house, locking the door upon the *outside*.

When Peter got home, his mother forgave him, because she was so glad to see that he had found his shoes and coat. Cotton-tail and Peter folded up the pocket-handkerchief, and old Mrs. Rabbit strung up the onions and hung them from the kitchen ceiling, with the bunches of herbs and the rabbit-tobacco.

THE END

THE TALE OF
TWO BAD MICE

1904

ABOUT THIS BOOK

The Tale of Two Bad Mice was written at a particularly happy time for Beatrix Potter: she and her editor, Norman Warne, were becoming firm friends, and Beatrix was sometimes included in Warne family celebrations. Norman made a new cage for Beatrix's pet mice, Tom Thumb and Hunca Munca, so that she could more easily draw them for her new book. He had also made a doll's house for his favourite niece, Winifred, and Beatrix was invited to visit and sketch this too. However, her mother objected, and so Beatrix had to make do with photographs and examples of doll's furniture and food that Norman sent her. She kept some of the furniture all her life, and it can still be seen at Hill Top, her first Lakeland home.

Beatrix dedicated the book to Winifred: "For W.M.L.W., the little girl who had the doll's house."

ONCE upon a time there was a very beautiful doll's-house; it was red brick with white windows, and it had real muslin curtains and a front door and a chimney.

It belonged to two Dolls called Lucinda and Jane, at least it belonged to Lucinda, but she never ordered meals.

Jane was the Cook; but she never did any cooking, because the dinner had been bought ready-made, in a box full of shavings.

There were two red lobsters and a ham, a fish, a pudding, and some pears and oranges.

They would not come off the plates, but they were extremely beautiful.

One morning Lucinda and Jane had gone out for a drive in the doll's perambulator. There was no one in the nursery, and it was very quiet. Presently there was a little scuffling, scratching noise in a corner near the fire-place, where there was a hole under the skirting-board.

Tom Thumb put out his head for a moment, and then popped it in again.

Tom Thumb was a mouse.

A minute afterwards, Hunca Munca, his wife, put her head out, too; and when she saw that there was no one in the nursery, she ventured out on the oilcloth under the coalbox.

The doll's-house stood at the other side of the fire-place. Tom Thumb and Hunca Munca went cautiously across the hearthrug. They pushed the front door—it was not fast.

Tom Thumb and Hunca Munca went upstairs and peeped into the dining-room. Then they squeaked with joy!

Such a lovely dinner was laid out upon the table! There were tin spoons, and lead knives and forks, and two dolly-chairs—all *so* convenient!

Tom Thumb set to work at once to carve the ham. It was a beautiful shiny yellow, streaked with red.

The knife crumpled up and hurt him; he put his finger in his mouth.

"It is not boiled enough; it is hard. You have a try, Hunca Munca."

Hunca Munca stood up in her chair, and chopped at the ham with another lead knife.

"It's as hard as the hams at the cheesemonger's," said Hunca Munca.

The ham broke off the plate with a jerk, and rolled under the table.

"Let it alone," said Tom Thumb; "give me some fish, Hunca Munca!"

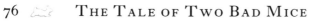

Hunca Munca tried every tin spoon in turn; the fish was glued to the dish.

Then Tom Thumb lost his temper. He put the ham in the middle of the floor, and hit it with the tongs and with the shovel—bang, bang, smash, smash!

The ham flew all into pieces, for underneath the shiny paint it was made of nothing but plaster!

Then there was no end to the rage and disappointment of Tom Thumb and Hunca Munca. They broke up the pudding, the lobsters, the pears and the oranges.

As the fish would not come off the plate, they put it into the red-hot crinkly paper fire in the kitchen; but it would not burn either.

Tom Thumb went up the kitchen chimney and looked out at the top—there was no soot.

While Tom Thumb was up the chimney, Hunca Munca had another disappointment. She found some tiny canisters upon the dresser, labelled—Rice—Coffee—Sago—but when she turned them upside down, there was nothing inside except red and blue beads.

Then those mice set to work to do all the mischief they could—especially Tom Thumb! He took Jane's clothes out of the chest of drawers in her bedroom, and he threw them out of the top floor window.

But Hunca Munca had a frugal mind. After pulling half the feathers out of Lucinda's bolster, she remembered that she herself was in want of a feather bed.

With Tom Thumb's assistance she carried the bolster downstairs, and across the hearthrug. It was difficult to squeeze the bolster into the mouse-hole; but they managed it somehow.

Then Hunca Munca went back and fetched a chair, a book-case, a bird-cage, and several small odds and ends. The book-case and the bird-cage refused to go into the mouse-hole.

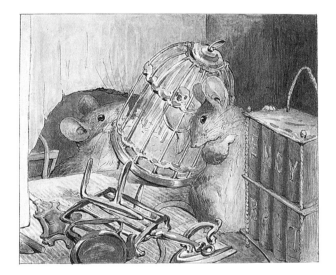

Hunca Munca left them behind the coal-box, and went to fetch a cradle.

Hunca Munca was just returning with another chair, when suddenly there was a noise of talking outside upon the landing. The mice rushed back to their hole, and the dolls came into the nursery.

What a sight met the eyes of Jane and Lucinda!

Lucinda sat upon the upset kitchen stove and stared; and Jane leant against the kitchen dresser and smiled—but neither of them made any remark.

The book-case and the bird-cage were rescued from under the coal-box—but Hunca Munca has got the cradle, and some of Lucinda's clothes.

She also has some useful pots and pans, and several other things.

The little girl that the doll's-house belonged to, said,—"I will get a doll dressed like a policeman!"

But the nurse said,—"I will set a mouse-trap!"

So that is the story of the two Bad Mice,—but they were not so very very naughty after all, because Tom Thumb paid for everything he broke.

He found a crooked sixpence under the hearthrug; and upon Christmas Eve, he and Hunca Munca stuffed it into one of the stockings of Lucinda and Jane.

And very early every morning—before anybody is awake—
Hunca Munca comes with her dust-pan and her broom to
sweep the Dollies' house!

THE END

THE TALE OF
MRS. TIGGY~WINKLE

1905

ABOUT THIS BOOK

Although many of Beatrix Potter's story-book animals were based on her own pets, she often gave them human qualities too. The character of Mrs. Tiggy-winkle was inspired by Kitty McDonald, an old Scottish washerwoman, "a comical, round little old woman, as brown as a berry and wears a multitude of petticoats". She first told the story to her cousin Stephanie Hyde Parker in 1901, though it was eventually dedicated on publication in 1905 to Lucie Carr, daughter of the Vicar of Newlands, the valley in which the tale is set. Beatrix's tame hedgehog, Mrs. Tiggy-winkle, did her duty as a model: "So long as she can go to sleep on my knee she is delighted, but if she is propped up on end for half an hour, she first begins to yawn pathetically, and then she *does* bite! Nevertheless she is a dear person."

ONCE upon a time there was a little girl called Lucie, who lived at a farm called Little-town. She was a good little girl—only she was always losing her pocket-handkerchiefs!

One day little Lucie came into the farm-yard crying—oh, she did cry so! "I've lost my pocket-handkin! Three handkins and a pinny! Have *you* seen them, Tabby Kitten?"

The kitten went on washing her white paws; so Lucie asked a speckled hen—
"Sally Henny-penny, have *you* found three pocket-handkins?"

But the speckled hen ran into a barn, clucking—
"I go barefoot, barefoot, barefoot!"

And then Lucie asked Cock Robin sitting on a twig.

Cock Robin looked sideways at Lucie with his bright black eye, and he flew over a stile and away.

Lucie climbed upon the stile and looked up at the hill behind Little-town—a hill that goes up—up—into the clouds as though it had no top!

And a great way up the hillside she thought she saw some white things spread upon the grass.

Lucie scrambled up the hill as fast as her stout legs would carry her; she ran along a steep path-way—up and up —until Little-town was right away down below—she could have dropped a pebble down the chimney!

Presently she came to a spring, bubbling out from the hill-side.

Someone had stood a tin can upon a stone to catch the water —but the water was already running over, for the can was no bigger than an egg-cup! And where the sand upon the path was wet—there were foot-marks of a *very* small person.

Lucie ran on, and on.

The path ended under a big rock. The grass was short and green, and there were clothes-props cut from bracken stems, with lines of plaited rushes, and a heap of tiny clothes pins—but no pocket-handkerchiefs!

But there was something else—a door! straight into the hill; and inside it some-one was singing—

"Lily-white and clean, oh!
With little frills between, oh!
Smooth and hot—red rusty spot
Never here be seen, oh!"

Lucie knocked—once—twice, and interrupted the song. A little frightened voice called out "Who's that?"

Lucie opened the door: and what do you think there was inside the hill?—a nice clean kitchen with a flagged floor and wooden beams—just like any other farm kitchen. Only the ceiling was so low that Lucie's head nearly touched it; and the pots and pans were small, and so was everything there.

There was a nice hot singey smell; and at the table, with an iron in her hand stood a very stout short person staring anxiously at Lucie.

Her print gown was tucked up, and she was wearing a large apron over her striped petticoat. Her little black nose went sniffle, sniffle, snuffle, and her eyes went twinkle, twinkle; and underneath her cap—where Lucie had yellow curls—that little person had PRICKLES!

"Who are you?" said Lucie. "Have you seen my pocket-handkins?"

The little person made a bob-curtsey—"Oh, yes, if you please'm; my name is Mrs. Tiggy-winkle; oh, yes if you please'm, I'm an excellent clear-starcher!" And she took something out of a clothes-basket, and spread it on the ironing-blanket.

"What's that thing?" said Lucie—"That's not my pocket-handkin?"

"Oh no, if you please'm; that's a little scarlet waist-coat belonging to Cock Robin!"

And she ironed it and folded it, and put it on one side.

Then she took something else off a clothes-horse—

"That isn't my pinny?" said Lucie.

"Oh no, if you please'm; that's a damask table-cloth belonging to Jenny Wren; look how it's stained with currant wine! It's very bad to wash!" said Mrs. Tiggy-winkle.

Mrs. Tiggy-winkle's nose went sniffle, sniffle, snuffle, and her eyes went twinkle, twinkle; and she fetched another hot iron from the fire.

"There's one of my pocket-
handkins!" cried Lucie—"And
there's my pinny!"

Mrs. Tiggy-winkle ironed it,
and goffered it, and shook out
the frills.

"Oh that *is* lovely!" said
Lucie.

"And what are those long
yellow things with fingers like
gloves?"

"Oh, that's a pair of
stockings belonging to Sally
Henny-penny—look how
she's worn the heels out
with scratching in the yard!
She'll very soon go barefoot!"
said Mrs. Tiggy-winkle.

"Why, there's another hand-kersniff—but it isn't mine; it's red?"

"Oh no, if you please'm; that one belongs to old Mrs. Rabbit; and it *did* so smell of onions! I've had to wash it separately, I can't get out the smell."

"There's another one of mine," said Lucie.

"What are those funny little white things?"

"That's a pair of mittens belonging to Tabby Kitten; I only have to iron them; she washes them herself."

"There's my last pocket-handkin!" said Lucie.

"And what are you dipping into the basin of starch?"
"They're little dicky shirt-fronts belonging to Tom Titmouse—most terrible particular!" said Mrs. Tiggy-winkle. "Now I've finished my ironing; I'm going to air some clothes."

"What are these dear soft fluffy things?" said Lucie.

"Oh those are woolly coats belonging to the little lambs at Skelghyl."

"Will their jackets take off?" asked Lucie.

"Oh yes, if you please'm; look at the sheep-mark on the shoulder. And here's one marked for Gatesgarth, and three that come from Little-town. They're *always* marked at washing!" said Mrs. Tiggy-winkle.

And she hung up all sorts and sizes of clothes—small brown coats of mice; and one velvety black mole-skin waist-coat; and a red tail-coat with no tail belonging to Squirrel Nutkin; and a very much shrunk blue jacket belonging to Peter Rabbit; and a petticoat, not marked, that had gone lost in the washing —and at last the basket was empty!

Then Mrs. Tiggy-winkle made tea—a cup for herself and a cup for Lucie. They sat before the fire on a bench and looked sideways at one another. Mrs. Tiggy-winkle's hand, holding the tea-cup, was very very brown, and very very wrinkly with the soap-suds; and all through her gown and her cap, there were *hair-pins* sticking wrong end out; so that Lucie didn't like to sit too near her.

When they had finished tea, they tied up the clothes in bundles; and Lucie's pocket-handkerchiefs were folded up inside her clean pinny, and fastened with a silver safety-pin.

And then they made up the fire with turf, and came out and locked the door, and hid the key under the door-sill.

Then away down the hill trotted Lucie and Mrs. Tiggy-winkle with the bundles of clothes!

All the way down the path little animals came out of the fern to meet them; the very first that they met were Peter Rabbit and Benjamin Bunny!

And she gave them their nice clean clothes; and all the little animals and birds were so very much obliged to dear Mrs. Tiggy-winkle.

So that at the bottom of the hill when they came to the stile, there was nothing left to carry except Lucie's one little bundle.

Lucie scrambled up the stile with the bundle in her hand; and then she turned to say "Good-night," and to thank the washer-woman—But what a *very* odd thing! Mrs. Tiggy-winkle had not waited either for thanks or for the washing bill!

She was running running running up the hill—and where was her white frilled cap? and her shawl? and her gown—and her petticoat?

And *how* small she had grown—and *how* brown—and covered with PRICKLES!

Why! Mrs. Tiggy-winkle was nothing but a HEDGEHOG.

* * * * *

(Now some people say that little Lucie had been asleep upon the stile—but then how could she have found three clean pocket-handkins and a pinny, pinned with a silver safety-pin?

And besides—*I* have seen that door into the back of the hill called Cat Bells—and besides *I* am very well acquainted with dear Mrs. Tiggy-winkle!)

THE END

THE TALE OF
THE PIE
AND THE PATTY-PAN

1905

ABOUT THIS BOOK

This story is rooted very firmly in the village of Sawrey, though Beatrix Potter was not yet living there when she sketched its lanes, houses and gardens in 1902. It was originally written in 1903, then laid aside until 1905. The tale reflects Beatrix's affection for the Lake District village and its inhabitants, and was one she was particularly pleased with: "If the book prints well it will be my next favourite to the *Tailor*." It was published in 1905, in a larger size than the other books, being reduced to the standard format in 1930 and listed as the seventeenth of *The Original Peter Rabbit Books*. The dedication reads, "For Joan [one of the Moore daughters], to read to Baby" [Beatrix's god-daughter, named after her, born in November 1903].

ONCE upon a time there was a Pussy-cat called Ribby, who invited a little dog called Duchess, to tea.

"Come in good time, my dear Duchess," said Ribby's letter, "and we will have something so very nice. I am baking it in a pie-dish—a pie-dish with a pink rim. You never tasted anything so good! And *you* shall eat it all! *I* will eat muffins, my dear Duchess!" wrote Ribby.

Duchess read the letter and wrote an answer:—"I will come with much pleasure at a quarter past four. But it is very strange. *I* was just going to invite you to come here, to supper, my dear Ribby, to eat something *most delicious.*

"I will come very punctually, my dear Ribby," wrote Duchess; and then at the end she added—"I hope it isn't mouse?"

And then she thought that did not look quite polite; so she scratched out "isn't mouse" and changed it to "I hope it will be fine," and she gave her letter to the postman.

But she thought a great deal about Ribby's pie, and she read Ribby's letter over and over again.

"I am dreadfully afraid it *will* be mouse!" said Duchess to herself—"I really couldn't, *couldn't* eat mouse pie. And I shall have to eat it, because it is a party. And *my* pie was going to be veal and ham. A pink and white pie-dish! and so is mine; just like Ribby's dishes; they were both bought at Tabitha Twitchit's."

Duchess went into her larder and took the pie off a shelf and looked at it.

"It is all ready to put into the oven. Such lovely pie-crust; and I put in a little tin patty-pan to hold up the crust; and I made a hole in the middle with a fork to let out the steam— Oh I do wish I could eat my own pie, instead of a pie made of mouse!"

Duchess considered and considered and read Ribby's letter again—

"A pink and white pie-dish—and *you* shall eat it *all*. 'You' means me—then Ribby is not going to even taste the pie herself? A pink and white pie-dish! Ribby is sure to go out to buy the muffins . . . Oh what a good idea! Why shouldn't I rush along and put my pie into Ribby's oven when Ribby isn't there?"

Duchess was quite delighted with her own cleverness!

Ribby in the meantime had received Duchess's answer, and as soon as she was sure that the little dog could come—she popped

her pie into the oven. There were two ovens, one above the other; some other knobs and handles were only ornamental and not intended to open. Ribby put the pie into the lower oven; the door was very stiff.

"The top oven bakes too quickly," said Ribby to herself. "It is a pie of the most delicate and tender mouse minced up with bacon. And I have taken out all the bones;

because Duchess did nearly choke herself with a fish-bone last time I gave a party. She eats a little fast— rather big mouthfuls. But a most genteel and elegant little dog; infinitely superior company to Cousin Tabitha Twitchit."

Ribby put on some coal and swept up the hearth. Then she went out with a can to the well, for water to fill up the kettle.

Then she began to set the room in order, for it was the sitting-room as well as the kitchen. She shook the mats out at the front door and put them straight; the hearth-rug was a rabbit-skin. She dusted the clock and the ornaments on the mantel-piece, and she polished and rubbed the tables and chairs.

Then she spread a very clean white table-cloth, and set out her best china tea-set, which she took out of a wall-cupboard near the fireplace.

The tea-cups were white with a pattern of pink roses; and the dinner-plates were white and blue.

When Ribby had laid the table she took a jug and a blue and white dish, and went out down the field to the farm, to fetch milk and butter.

When she came back, she peeped into the bottom oven; the pie looked very comfortable.

Ribby put on her shawl and bonnet and went out again with a basket, to the village

shop to buy a packet of tea, a pound of lump sugar, and a pot of marmalade.

And just at the same time, Duchess came out of *her* house, at the other end of the village.

Ribby met Duchess half-way down the street, also carrying a basket, covered with a cloth. They only bowed to one another;

they did not speak, because they were going to have a party.

As soon as Duchess had got round the corner out of sight—she simply ran! Straight away to Ribby's house!

Ribby went into the shop and bought what she required, and came out, after a pleasant gossip with Cousin Tabitha Twitchit.

Cousin Tabitha was disdainful afterwards in conversation—

"A little *dog* indeed! Just as if there were no CATS in Sawrey! And a *pie* for afternoon tea! The very idea!" said Cousin Tabitha Twitchit.

Ribby went on to Timothy Baker's and bought the muffins. Then she went home.

There seemed to be a sort of scuffling noise in the back passage, as she was coming in at the front door.

"I trust that is not that Pie: the spoons are locked up, however," said Ribby.

But there was nobody there. Ribby opened the bottom oven door with some difficulty, and turned the pie. There began to be a pleasing smell of baked mouse!

Duchess in the meantime, had slipped out at the back door.

"It is a very odd thing that Ribby's pie was *not* in the oven when I put mine in! And I can't find it anywhere; I have looked all over the house. I put *my* pie into a nice hot oven at the top. I could not turn any of the other handles; I think that they are all shams," said Duchess, "but I wish I could have removed the pie made of mouse! I cannot think what she has done with it? I heard Ribby coming and I had to run out by the back door!"

Duchess went home and brushed her beautiful black coat; and then she picked a bunch of flowers in her garden as a present for Ribby; and passed the time until the clock struck four.

Ribby—having assured herself by careful search that there was really no one hiding in the cupboard or in the larder—went upstairs to change her dress.

She put on a lilac silk gown, for the party, and an embroidered muslin apron and tippet.

"It is very strange," said Ribby, "I did not *think* I left that drawer pulled out; has some-body been trying on my mittens?"

She came downstairs again, and made the tea, and put the teapot on the hob. She peeped again into the *bottom* oven, the pie had become a lovely brown, and it was steaming hot.

She sat down before the fire to wait for the little dog. "I am glad I used the *bottom* oven," said Ribby, "the top one would certainly have been very much too hot. I wonder why that cupboard door was open? Can there really have been someone in the house?"

Very punctually at four o'clock, Duchess started to go to the party. She ran so fast through the village that she was too early, and she had to wait a little while in the lane that leads down to Ribby's house.

"I wonder if Ribby has taken *my* pie out of the oven yet?" said Duchess, "and whatever can have become of the other pie made of mouse?"

At a quarter past four to the minute, there came a most genteel little tap-tappity. "Is Mrs. Ribston at home?" inquired Duchess in the porch.

"Come in! and how do you do, my dear Duchess?" cried Ribby. "I hope I see you well?"

"Quite well, I thank you, and how do *you* do, my dear Ribby?" said Duchess. "I've brought you some flowers; what a delicious smell of pie!"

"Oh, what lovely flowers! Yes, it is mouse and bacon!"

"Do not talk about food, my dear Ribby," said Duchess; "what a lovely white tea-cloth! . . . Is it done to a turn? Is it still in the oven?"

"I think it wants another five minutes," said Ribby. "Just a shade longer; I will pour out the tea, while we wait. Do you take sugar, my dear Duchess?"

"Oh yes, please! my dear Ribby; and may I have a lump upon my nose?"

"With pleasure, my dear Duchess; how beautifully you beg! Oh, how sweetly pretty!"

Duchess sat up with the sugar on her nose and sniffed—

"How good that pie smells! I do love veal and ham—I mean to say mouse and bacon—"

She dropped the sugar in confusion, and had to go hunting under the tea-table, so did not see which oven Ribby opened in order to get out the pie.

Ribby set the pie upon the table; there was a very savoury smell.

Duchess came out from under the table-cloth munching sugar, and sat up on a chair.

"I will first cut the pie for you; I am going to have muffin and marmalade," said Ribby.

"Do you really prefer muffin? Mind the patty-pan!"

"I beg your pardon?" said Ribby.

"May I pass you the marmalade?" said Duchess hurriedly.

The pie proved extremely toothsome, and the muffins light and hot. They disappeared rapidly, especially the pie!

"I think"—(thought the Duchess to herself)—"I *think* it would be wiser if I helped myself to pie; though Ribby did not seem to notice anything when she was cutting it. What very small fine pieces it has cooked into! I did not remember that I had minced it up so fine; I suppose this is a quicker oven than my own."

"How fast Duchess is eating!" thought Ribby to herself, as she buttered her fifth muffin.

The pie-dish was emptying rapidly! Duchess had had four helps already, and was fumbling with the spoon.

"A little more bacon, my dear Duchess?" said Ribby.

"Thank you, my dear Ribby; I was only feeling for the patty-pan."

"The patty-pan? my dear Duchess?"

"The patty-pan that held up the pie-crust," said Duchess, blushing under her black coat.

"Oh, I didn't put one in, my dear Duchess," said Ribby; "I don't think that it is necessary in pies made of mouse."

Duchess fumbled with the spoon—"I can't find it!" she said anxiously.

"There isn't a patty-pan," said Ribby, looking perplexed.

"Yes, indeed, my dear Ribby; where can it have gone to?" said Duchess.

"There most certainly is not one, my dear Duchess. I disapprove of tin articles in puddings and pies. It is most

undesirable—(especially when people swallow in lumps!)" she added in a lower voice.

Duchess looked very much alarmed, and continued to scoop the inside of the pie-dish.

"My Great-aunt Squintina (grandmother of Cousin Tabitha Twitchit) —died of a thimble in a Christmas plum-pudding. *I* never put any article of metal in *my* puddings or pies."

Duchess looked aghast, and tilted up the pie-dish.

"I have only four patty-pans, and they are all in the cupboard."

Duchess set up a howl.

"I shall die! I shall die! I have swallowed a patty-pan! Oh, my dear Ribby, I do feel so ill!"

"It is impossible, my dear Duchess; there was not a patty-pan."

Duchess moaned and whined and rocked herself about.

"Oh I feel so dreadful, I have swallowed a patty-pan!"

"There was *nothing* in the pie," said Ribby severely.

"Yes there *was,* my dear Ribby, I am sure I have swallowed it!"

"Let me prop you up with a pillow, my dear Duchess; where do you think you feel it?"

"Oh I do feel so ill *all over* me, my dear Ribby; I have swallowed a large tin patty-pan with a sharp scalloped edge!"

"Shall I run for the doctor? I will just lock up the spoons!"

"Oh yes, yes! fetch Dr. Maggotty, my dear Ribby: he is a Pie himself, he will certainly understand."

Ribby settled Duchess in an armchair before the fire, and went out and hurried to the village to look for the doctor.

She found him at the smithy.

He was occupied in putting rusty nails into a bottle of ink, which he had obtained at the post office.

"Gammon? ha! HA!" said he, with his head on one side.

Ribby explained that her guest had swallowed a patty-pan.

"Spinach? ha! HA!" said he, and accompanied her with alacrity.

He hopped so fast that Ribby had to run. It was most conspicuous. All the village could see that Ribby was fetching the doctor.

"I *knew* that they would over-eat themselves!" said Cousin Tabitha Twitchit.

But while Ribby had been hunting for the doctor—a curious thing had happened to Duchess, who had been left by herself, sitting before the fire, sighing and groaning and feeling very unhappy.

"How *could* I have swallowed it! such a large thing as a patty-pan!"

She got up and went to the table, and felt inside the pie-dish again with a spoon.

"No; there is no patty-pan, and I put one in; and nobody has eaten pie except me, so I must have swallowed it!"

She sat down again, and stared mournfully at the grate. The fire crackled and danced, and something sizz-z-zled!

Duchess started! She opened the door of the *top* oven;—out came a rich steamy flavour of veal and ham, and there stood a fine brown pie,—and through a hole in the top of the pie-crust there was a glimpse of a little tin patty-pan!

Duchess drew a long breath—

"Then I must have been eating MOUSE! . . .   No wonder I feel ill . . .   But perhaps I should feel worse if I had really swallowed a patty-pan!" Duchess reflected—"What a very awkward thing to have to explain to Ribby! I think I will put *my* pie in the back-yard and say nothing about it. When I go home, I will run round and take it away." She put it outside

the back-door, and sat down again by the fire, and shut her eyes; when Ribby arrived with the doctor, she seemed fast asleep.

"Gammon, ha, HA?" said the doctor.

"I am feeling very much better," said Duchess, waking up with a jump.

"I am truly glad to hear it! He has brought you a pill, my dear Duchess!"

"I think I should feel *quite* well if he only felt my pulse," said Duchess, backing away from the magpie, who sidled up with something in his beak.

"It is only a bread pill, you had much better take it; drink a little milk, my dear Duchess!"

"Gammon? Gammon?" said the doctor, while Duchess coughed and choked.

"Don't say that again!" said Ribby, losing her temper—"Here, take this bread and jam, and get out into the yard!"

"Gammon and Spinach! ha ha HA!" shouted Dr. Maggotty triumphantly outside the back door.

"I am feeling very much better my dear Ribby," said Duchess. "Do you not think that I had better go home before it gets dark?"

"Perhaps it might be wise, my dear Duchess. I will lend you a nice warm shawl, and you shall take my arm."

"I would not trouble you for worlds; I feel wonderfully better. One pill of Dr. Maggotty—"

"Indeed it is most admirable, if it has cured you of a patty-pan! I will call directly after breakfast to ask how you have slept."

Ribby and Duchess said goodbye affectionately, and Duchess started home. Half-way up the lane she stopped and looked back; Ribby had gone in and shut her door. Duchess slipped through the fence, and ran round to the back of Ribby's house, and peeped into the yard.

Upon the roof of the pig-stye sat Dr. Maggotty and three jackdaws. The jackdaws were eating pie-crust, and the magpie was drinking gravy out of a patty-pan.

"Gammon, ha, HA!" he shouted when he saw Duchess's little black nose peeping round the corner.

Duchess ran home feeling uncommonly silly!

When Ribby came out for a pailful of water to wash up the tea-things, she found a pink and white pie-dish lying smashed in the middle of the yard. The patty-pan was under the pump, where Dr. Maggotty had considerately left it.

Ribby stared with amazement—"Did you ever see the like! So there really *was* a patty-pan? . . . But *my* patty-pans are all in the kitchen cupboard. Well I never did! . . . Next time I want to give a party—I will invite Cousin Tabitha Twitchit!"

THE END

THE TALE OF
MR. JEREMY FISHER

1906

About This Book

Mr. Jeremy Fisher had existed in Beatrix Potter's imagination for many years before his story was eventually published in 1906. He first appeared in 1893 in a picture letter to Eric Moore, written by Beatrix the day after she had sent the Peter Rabbit story to his brother Noel. In 1894, she produced a series of black-and-white frog drawings which were published in a children's annual and in 1902, Beatrix discussed Mr. Jeremy with her editor, Norman Warne. After Norman's death in 1905, Beatrix needed to work and took up the story with Harold, Norman's brother, as her new editor. "I feel as if my work and your kindness will be my greatest comfort." Perhaps the solitary hours spent sketching tranquil scenes in the Lake District did bring Beatrix comfort: the book certainly contains some of her most beautiful paintings. It is dedicated to Stephanie Hyde Parker, "from Cousin B."

ONCE upon a time there was a frog called Mr. Jeremy Fisher; he lived in a little damp house amongst the buttercups at the edge of a pond.

The water was all slippy-sloppy in the larder and in the back passage.

But Mr. Jeremy liked getting his feet wet; nobody ever scolded him, and he never caught a cold!

He was quite pleased when he looked out and saw large drops of rain, splashing in the pond—

"I will get some worms and go fishing
and catch a dish of minnows for my
dinner," said Mr. Jeremy Fisher.
"If I catch more than five fish,
I will invite my friends Mr.
Alderman Ptolemy Tortoise
and Sir Isaac Newton. The
Alderman, however, eats salad."

Mr. Jeremy put on a
macintosh, and a pair of shiny
goloshes;

he took his rod and basket, and
set off with enormous hops to
the place where he kept his boat.

The boat was round and green,
and very like the other lily-leaves.
It was tied to a water-plant in the
middle of the pond.

Mr. Jeremy took a reed pole, and pushed the boat out into open water. "I know a good place for minnows," said Mr. Jeremy Fisher.

Mr. Jeremy stuck his pole into the mud and fastened his boat to it.

Then he settled himself cross-legged and arranged his fishing tackle.

He had the dearest little red float. His rod was a tough stalk of grass, his line was a fine long white horse-hair,

and he tied a little wriggling worm at the end.

The rain trickled down his back, and for nearly an hour he stared at the float.

"This is getting tiresome, I think I should like some lunch," said Mr. Jeremy Fisher.

He punted back again amongst the water-plants, and took some lunch out of his basket.

"I will eat a butterfly sandwich, and wait till the shower is over," said Mr. Jeremy Fisher.

A great big water-beetle came up underneath the lily leaf and tweaked the toe of one of his goloshes.

Mr. Jeremy crossed his legs up shorter, out of reach, and went on eating his sandwich.

Once or twice something moved about with a rustle and a splash amongst the rushes at the side of the pond.

"I trust that is not a rat," said Mr. Jeremy Fisher; "I think I had better get away from here."

Mr. Jeremy shoved the boat out again a little way, and dropped in the bait. There was a bite almost directly; the float gave a tremendous bobbit!

"A minnow! A minnow! I have him by the nose!" cried Mr. Jeremy Fisher, jerking up his rod.

But what a horrible surprise! Instead of a smooth fat minnow, Mr. Jeremy landed little Jack Sharp the stickle-back, covered with spines!

The stickleback floundered about the boat, pricking and snapping until he was quite out of breath.

Then he jumped back into the water.

And a shoal of other little fishes put their heads out, and laughed at Mr. Jeremy Fisher.

And while Mr. Jeremy sat
disconsolately on the edge of his
boat—sucking his sore fingers and
peering down into the water—
a *much* worse thing happened;
a really *frightful* thing it would
have been, if Mr. Jeremy had
not been wearing a macintosh!

A great big enormous trout
came up—ker-pflop-p-p-p!
with a splash—

—and it seized Mr. Jeremy
with a snap, "Ow! Ow! Ow!"
—and then it turned and dived
down to the bottom of the pond!

But the trout was so displeased
with the taste of the macintosh,
that in less than half a minute it spat
him out again; and the only thing it
swallowed was Mr. Jeremy's goloshes.

Mr. Jeremy bounced up to the surface of the water, like a cork and the bubbles out of a soda water bottle; and he swam with all his might to the edge of the pond.

He scrambled out on the first bank he came to, and he hopped home across the meadow with his macintosh all in tatters.

"What a mercy that was not a pike!" said Mr. Jeremy Fisher.

"I have lost my rod and basket; but it does not much matter, for I am sure I should never have dared to go fishing again!"

He put some sticking plaster on his fingers, and his friends both came to dinner. He could not offer them fish, but he had something else in his larder.

Sir Isaac Newton wore his black and gold waistcoat.

And Mr. Alderman Ptolemy Tortoise brought a salad with him in a string bag.

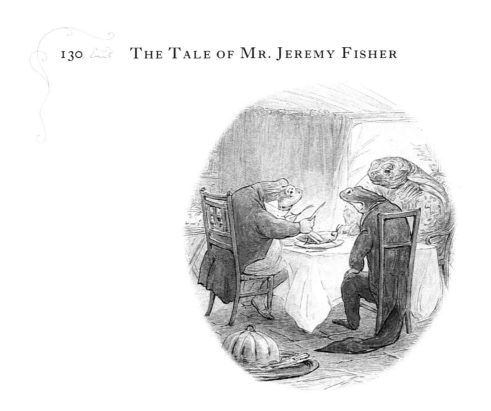

And instead of a nice dish of minnows—they had a roasted grasshopper with lady-bird sauce; which frogs consider a beautiful treat; but *I* think it must have been nasty!

THE END

THE STORY OF
A FIERCE BAD RABBIT

1906

ABOUT THIS BOOK

The Story of A Fierce Bad Rabbit, together with *The Story of Miss Moppet*, was first published as a panorama, unfolding in a long strip of pictures and text from a wallet with a tuck-in flap. Both books were intended for very young children; *The Story of A Fierce Bad Rabbit* had been written especially for editor Harold Warne's little daughter, Louie, who had told Beatrix that Peter was too good a rabbit, and she wanted a story about a *really* naughty one!

Unfortunately the panoramic format was not popular with the bookshops. As Beatrix wrote later: "The shops sensibly refused to stock them because they got unrolled and so bad to roll up again." In 1916, both stories were reprinted in book form and listed at the end of the series of Peter Rabbit books, alongside the nursery rhyme collections which were also intended for the very young.

THIS is a fierce bad Rabbit; look at his savage whiskers, and his claws and his turned-up tail.

This is a nice gentle Rabbit. His mother has given him a carrot.

The bad Rabbit would like some carrot.

He doesn't say "Please."
He takes it!

And he scratches the
good Rabbit very badly.

The good Rabbit
creeps away, and hides
in a hole. It feels sad.

This is a man with a gun.

He sees something sitting on a bench. He thinks it is a very funny bird!

He comes creeping up behind the trees.

And then he shoots—
BANG!

This is what happens—

But this is all he finds on
the bench, when he rushes
up with his gun.

The good Rabbit
peeps out of its hole.

And it sees the bad
Rabbit tearing past—
without any tail or
whiskers!

THE END

THE STORY OF
MISS MOPPET

1906

About This Book

The Story of Miss Moppet was the second book to be published as a fold-out concertina (alongside *The Story of A Fierce Bad Rabbit*), in time for Christmas 1906. Moppet is Tom Kitten's sister, and the simple story about her exploits with a cheeky mouse is intended for very young children. Beatrix Potter did not want to upset her young audience unduly, writing on the draft for one picture, "She should catch him by the tail – less unpleasant." All ends happily in this delightful story, however.

The book was reprinted in a standard format in 1916 to please the bookshops, and listed at the end of the series of Peter Rabbit books with the other three titles for very young children, *The Story of A Fierce Bad Rabbit,* and *Appley Dapply's* and *Cecily Parsley's Nursery Rhymes.*

THIS is a Pussy called
Miss Moppet, she
thinks she has heard a
mouse!

This is the Mouse peeping
out behind the cupboard,
and making fun of Miss
Moppet. He is not afraid of
a kitten.

This is Miss Moppet jumping just too late; she misses the Mouse and hits her own head.

She thinks it is a very hard cupboard!

The Mouse watches Miss Moppet from the top of the cupboard.

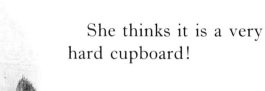

Miss Moppet ties up her head in a duster, and sits before the fire.

The Mouse thinks she is looking very ill. He comes sliding down the bell-pull.

Miss Moppet looks worse and worse. The Mouse comes a little nearer.

Miss Moppet holds her poor head in her paws, and looks at him through a hole in the duster. The Mouse comes *very* close.

And then all of a sudden— Miss Moppet jumps upon the Mouse!

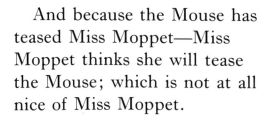

And because the Mouse has teased Miss Moppet—Miss Moppet thinks she will tease the Mouse; which is not at all nice of Miss Moppet.

She ties him up in the duster, and tosses it about like a ball.

But she forgot about that hole in the duster; and when she untied it —there was no Mouse!

He has wriggled out and run away; and he is dancing a jig on the top of the cupboard!

THE END

THE TALE OF
TOM KITTEN

1907

ABOUT THIS BOOK

By the time Beatrix Potter started writing *The Tale of Tom Kitten*, she had owned Hill Top farm, in the Lake District village of Sawrey, for a year. The expansion of the farmhouse was finished, and Beatrix was enthusiastically planning her cottage garden. She could not completely desert her property for writing, and both house and garden feature in the story. Mrs. Tabitha Twitchit leads her children up the path to Hill Top's front door, while inside we see its staircase and bedrooms. The kittens romp through the garden's flowers to jump up on the wall overlooking Sawrey, and the ducks march across the farmyard.

Beatrix used the same kitten as a model for both Miss Moppet and Tom. "It is very young and pretty and a most fearful pickle." She dedicated this story to "all Pickles – especially to those that get upon my garden wall."

ONCE upon a time there were three little kittens, and their names were Mittens, Tom Kitten, and Moppet.

They had dear little fur coats of their own; and they tumbled about the doorstep and played in the dust.

But one day their mother—Mrs. Tabitha Twitchit—expected friends to tea; so she fetched the kittens indoors, to wash and dress them, before the fine company arrived.

First she scrubbed their faces (this one is Moppet).

Then she brushed their fur (this one is Mittens).

Then she combed their tails and whiskers (this is Tom Kitten).

Tom was very naughty, and he scratched.

Mrs. Tabitha dressed
Moppet and Mittens in
clean pinafores and
tuckers; and then she
took all sorts of elegant
uncomfortable clothes
out of a chest of drawers,
in order to dress up her
son Thomas.

Tom Kitten was very fat, and
he had grown; several buttons
burst off. His mother sewed
them on again.

When the three kittens were
ready, Mrs. Tabitha unwisely
turned them out into the garden,
to be out of the way while she
made hot buttered toast.

"Now keep your frocks clean,
children! You must walk on your

hind legs. Keep away from the dirty ash-pit, and from Sally Henny Penny, and from the pig-stye and the Puddle-ducks."

Moppet and Mittens walked down the garden path unsteadily. Presently they trod upon their pinafores and fell on their noses. When they stood up there were several green smears!

"Let us climb up the rockery, and sit on the garden wall," said Moppet.

They turned their pinafores back to front, and went up with a skip and a jump; Moppet's white tucker fell down into the road.

Tom Kitten was quite unable to jump when walking upon his hind legs in trousers. He came up the rockery by degrees, breaking the ferns, and shedding buttons right and left.

He was all in pieces when he reached the top of the wall.

Moppet and Mittens tried to pull him together; his hat fell off, and the rest of his buttons burst.

While they were in difficulties, there was a pit pat paddle pat! and the three Puddle-ducks came along the hard high road, marching one behind the other and doing the goose step— pit pat paddle pat! Pit pat waddle pat!

They stopped and stood in a row, and stared up at the kittens. They had very small eyes and looked surprised.

Then the two duck-birds, Rebeccah and Jemima Puddle-duck, picked up the hat and tucker and put them on.

Mittens laughed so that she fell off the wall. Moppet and Tom descended after her; the pinafores and all the rest of Tom's clothes came off on the way down.

"Come! Mr. Drake Puddle-duck," said Moppet—"Come and help us to dress him! Come and button up Tom!"

Mr. Drake Puddle-duck advanced in a slow sideways manner, and picked up the various articles.

But he put them on *himself!* They fitted him even worse than Tom Kitten.

"It's a very fine morning!" said Mr. Drake Puddle-duck.

And he and Jemima and Rebeccah Puddle-duck set off up the road, keeping step— pit pat, paddle pat! Pit pat, waddle pat!

Then Tabitha Twitchit came down the garden and found her kittens on the wall with no clothes on.

She pulled them off the wall, smacked them, and took them back to the house.

"My friends will arrive in a minute, and you are not fit to be seen; I am affronted," said Mrs. Tabitha Twitchit.

She sent them upstairs; and I am sorry to say she told her friends that they were in bed with the measles; which was not true.

Quite the contrary; they were not in bed: *not* in the least.

Somehow there were very extraordinary noises over-head, which disturbed the dignity and repose of the tea party.

And I think that some day I shall have to make another, larger, book, to tell you more about Tom Kitten!

As for the Puddle-ducks— they went into a pond.

The clothes all came off directly, because there were no buttons.

And Mr. Drake Puddle-duck, and Jemima and Rebeccah, have been looking for them ever since.

THE END

The Tale of Jemima Puddle~Duck

1908

ABOUT THIS BOOK

Beatrix Potter's love of Hill Top and farming shine through this story. She painted her farm manager's wife, Mrs. Cannon, feeding the poultry, while the children Ralph and Betsy (to whom this "farmyard tale" is dedicated) are also illustrated. Kep the collie was Beatrix's favourite sheepdog, and Jemima herself was a real duck who lived at Hill Top. She is a most popular character: self-important, naive, but very endearing.

The story also contains many delightful views of Sawrey: Jemima's wood can still be seen, the view from the hills above the farm, across Esthwaite Water, has not changed, and the Tower Bank Arms is still the local village pub. This blend of fantasy and reality, so often to be found in Beatrix Potter's work, gives a ring of truth to her imaginary world.

WHAT a funny sight it is to see a brood of ducklings with a hen!
—Listen to the story of Jemima Puddle-duck, who was annoyed because the farmer's wife would not let her hatch her own eggs.

Her sister-in-law, Mrs. Rebeccah Puddle-duck, was perfectly willing to leave the hatching to someone else— "I have not the patience to sit on a nest for twenty-eight days; and no more have you, Jemima. You would let them go cold; you know you would!"

"I wish to hatch my own eggs; I will hatch them all by myself," quacked Jemima Puddle-duck.

She tried to hide her eggs;
but they were always found
and carried off.

Jemima Puddle-duck became
quite desperate. She determined
to make a nest right away from
the farm.

She set off on a fine spring
afternoon along the cart-road
that leads over the hill.

She was wearing a shawl and
a poke bonnet.

When she reached the top
of the hill, she saw a wood
in the distance.

She thought that it looked
a safe quiet spot.

Jemima Puddle-duck was not much in the habit of flying. She ran downhill a few yards flapping her shawl, and then she jumped off into the air.

She flew beautifully when she had got a good start.

She skimmed along over the tree-tops until she saw an open place in the middle of the wood, where the trees and brushwood had been cleared.

Jemima alighted rather heavily, and began to waddle about in search of a convenient dry nesting-place.

She rather fancied a tree-stump amongst some tall fox-gloves.

But—seated upon the stump, she was startled to find an elegantly dressed gentleman reading a newspaper.

He had black prick ears and sandy-coloured whiskers.

"Quack?" said Jemima Puddle-duck, with her head and her bonnet on one side— "Quack?"

The gentleman raised his eyes above his newspaper and looked curiously at Jemima—

"Madam, have you lost your way?" said he. He had a long bushy tail which he was sitting upon, as the stump was somewhat damp.

Jemima thought him mighty civil and handsome. She explained that she had not lost her way, but that she was trying to find a convenient dry nesting-place.

"Ah! Is that so? Indeed!" said the gentleman with sandy whiskers, looking curiously at Jemima. He folded up the newspaper, and put it in his coat-tail pocket.

Jemima complained of the superfluous hen.

"Indeed! How interesting!

I wish I could meet with that fowl. I would teach it to mind its own business!

"But as to a nest—there is no difficulty: I have a sackful of feathers in my woodshed. No, my dear madam, you will be in nobody's way. You may sit there as long as you like," said the bushy long-tailed gentleman.

He led the way to a very retired, dismal-looking house amongst the fox-gloves.

It was built of faggots and turf, and there were two broken pails, one on top of another, by way of a chimney.

"This is my summer residence; you would not find my earth—my winter house—so convenient," said the hospitable gentleman.

There was a tumble-down shed at the back of the house, made of old soap-boxes. The gentleman opened the door, and showed Jemima in.

The shed was almost quite full of feathers—it was almost suffocating; but it was comfortable and very soft.

Jemima Puddle-duck was rather surprised to find such a vast quantity of feathers. But it was very comfortable; and she made a nest without any trouble at all.

When she came out, the sandy-whiskered gentleman was sitting on a log reading the newspaper—at least he had it spread out, but he was looking over the top of it.

He was so polite, that he seemed almost sorry to let Jemima go home for the night. He promised to take great care of her nest until she came back again next day.

He said he loved eggs and ducklings; he should be proud to see a fine nestful in his wood-shed.

Jemima Puddle-duck came every afternoon; she laid nine eggs in the nest. They were greeny white and very large. The

foxy gentleman admired them immensely. He used to turn them over and count them when Jemima was not there.

At last Jemima told him that she intended to begin to sit next day—"and I will bring a bag of corn with me, so that I need never leave my nest until the eggs are hatched. They might catch cold," said the conscientious Jemima.

"Madam, I beg you not to trouble yourself with a bag; I will provide oats. But before you commence your tedious sitting, I intend to give you a treat. Let us have a dinner-party all to ourselves! May I ask you to bring up some herbs from the farm-garden to make a savoury omelette? Sage and thyme, and mint and two onions, and some parsley. I will provide lard for the stuff—

lard for the omelette," said the hospitable gentleman with sandy whiskers.

Jemima Puddle-duck was a simpleton: not even the mention of sage and onions made her suspicious.

She went round the farm-garden, nibbling off snippets of all the different sorts of herbs that are used for stuffing roast duck.

And she waddled into the kitchen, and got two onions out of a basket.

The collie-dog Kep met her coming out. "What are you doing with those onions? Where do you go every afternoon by yourself, Jemima Puddle-duck?"

Jemima was rather in awe of the collie; she told him the whole story.

The collie listened, with his wise head on one side; he grinned when she described the polite gentleman with sandy whiskers.

He asked several questions about the wood, and about the exact position of the house and shed.

Then he went out, and trotted down the village. He went to look for two fox-hound puppies who were out at walk with the butcher.

Jemima Puddle-duck went up the cart-road for the last time, on a sunny afternoon. She was rather burdened with bunches of herbs and two onions in a bag.

She flew over the wood, and alighted opposite the house of the bushy long-tailed gentleman.

He was sitting on a log; he sniffed the air, and kept glancing uneasily round the wood. When Jemima alighted he quite jumped.

"Come into the house as soon as you have looked at your eggs. Give me the herbs for the omelette. Be sharp!"

He was rather abrupt. Jemima Puddle-duck had never heard him speak like that.

She felt surprised, and uncomfortable.

While she was inside she heard pattering feet round the back of the shed. Some-one with a black nose sniffed at the bottom of the door, and then locked it.

Jemima became much alarmed.

A moment afterwards there were most awful noises—barking, baying, growls and howls, squealing and groans.

And nothing more was ever seen of that foxy-whiskered gentleman.

Presently Kep opened the door of the shed, and let out Jemima Puddle-duck.

Unfortunately the puppies rushed in and gobbled up all the eggs before he could stop them.

He had a bite on his ear and both the puppies were limping. Jemima Puddle-duck was escorted home in tears on account of those eggs.

She laid some more in June, and she was permitted to keep them herself: but only four of them hatched.

Jemima Puddle-duck said that it was because of her nerves; but she had always been a bad sitter.

THE END

THE TALE OF
SAMUEL WHISKERS
OR
THE ROLY-POLY PUDDING

1908

ABOUT THIS BOOK

When this story was first published in 1908, it was entitled *The Roly-Poly Pudding*, and appeared in the larger size used for *The Pie and The Patty-Pan*. In 1926 it was reduced to the standard size and given the title we now know it by.

The tale was actually written in 1906, when Beatrix was exploring Hill Top, the farm she had recently bought. She described the house in a letter to a friend. "It really is delightful – if the rats could be stopped out! . . . I never saw such a place for hide and seek and funny cupboards and closets." Here was her inspiration for the further adventures of Tom Kitten: an old farmhouse, and her pet rat, to whom the book is dedicated, "In remembrance of Sammy, the intelligent pink-eyed representative of a persecuted (but irrepressible) race. An affectionate little friend, and most accomplished thief."

ONCE upon a time there was an old cat, called Mrs. Tabitha Twitchit, who was an anxious parent. She used to lose her kittens continually, and whenever they were lost they were always in mischief!

On baking day she determined to shut them up in a cupboard.

She caught Moppet and Mittens, but she could not find Tom.

Mrs. Tabitha went up and down all over the house,  mewing for Tom Kitten. She looked in the pantry under the staircase, and she searched the best spare bedroom that was all covered up with dust sheets. She went right upstairs and looked into the attics, but she could not find him anywhere.

It was an old, old house, full of cupboards and passages. Some of the walls were four feet thick, and there used to be queer noises inside them, as if there might be a little secret staircase. Certainly there were odd little jagged doorways in the wainscot, and things disappeared at night—especially cheese and bacon.

Mrs. Tabitha became more and more distracted, and mewed dreadfully.

While their mother was searching the house, Moppet and Mittens had got into mischief.

The cupboard door was not locked, so they pushed it open and came out.

They went straight to the dough which was set to rise in a pan before the fire.

They patted it with their little soft paws—"Shall we make dear little muffins?" said Mittens to Moppet.

But just at that moment somebody knocked at the front door, and Moppet jumped into the flour barrel in a fright.

Mittens ran away to the dairy, and hid in an empty jar on the stone shelf where the milk pans stand.

The visitor was a neighbour, Mrs. Ribby; she had called to borrow some yeast.

Mrs. Tabitha came downstairs mewing dreadfully—"Come in, Cousin Ribby, come in, and sit ye down! I'm in sad trouble, Cousin Ribby," said Tabitha, shedding tears. "I've lost my dear son Thomas; I'm afraid the rats have got him." She wiped her eyes with her apron.

"He's a bad kitten, Cousin Tabitha; he made a cat's cradle of my best bonnet last time I came to tea. Where have you looked for him?"

"All over the house! The rats are too many for me. What a thing it is to have an unruly family!" said Mrs. Tabitha Twitchit.

"I'm not afraid of rats; I will help you to find him; and whip him too! What is all that soot in the fender?"

"The chimney wants sweeping—Oh, dear me, Cousin Ribby—now Moppet and Mittens are gone!

"They have both got out of the cupboard!"

Ribby and Tabitha set to work to search the house thoroughly again. They poked under the beds with Ribby's umbrella, and they rummaged in cupboards. They even fetched a candle, and looked inside a

clothes chest in one of the attics. They could not find anything, but once they heard a door bang and somebody scuttered downstairs.

"Yes, it is infested with rats," said Tabitha tearfully. "I caught seven young ones out of one hole in the back kitchen, and we had them for dinner last Saturday. And once I saw the old father rat —an enormous old rat, Cousin Ribby. I was just going to jump upon him, when he showed his yellow teeth at me and whisked down the hole.

"The rats get upon my nerves, Cousin Ribby," said Tabitha.

Ribby and Tabitha searched and searched.

They both heard a curious roly-poly noise under the attic floor. But there was nothing to be seen.

They returned to the kitchen. "Here's one of your kittens at least," said Ribby, dragging Moppet out of the flour barrel.

They shook the flour off her and set her down on the kitchen floor. She seemed to be in a terrible fright.

"Oh! Mother, Mother," said Moppet, "there's been an old woman rat in the kitchen, and she's stolen some of the dough!"

The two cats ran to look at the dough pan. Sure enough there

were marks of little scratching fingers, and a lump of dough was gone!

"Which way did she go, Moppet?"

But Moppet had been too much frightened to peep out of the barrel again.

Ribby and Tabitha took her with them to keep her safely in sight, while they went on with their search.

They went into the dairy.

The first thing they found was Mittens, hiding in an empty jar.

They tipped up the jar, and she scrambled out.

"Oh, Mother, Mother!" said Mittens—

"Oh! Mother, Mother, there has been an old man rat in the dairy— a dreadful 'normous big rat, Mother; and he's stolen a pat of butter and the rolling-pin."

Ribby and Tabitha looked at one another.

"A rolling-pin and butter! Oh, my poor son Thomas!" exclaimed Tabitha, wringing her paws.

"A rolling-pin?" said Ribby. "Did we not hear a roly-poly noise in the attic when we were looking into that chest?"

Ribby and Tabitha rushed upstairs again. Sure enough the roly-poly noise was still going on quite distinctly under the attic floor.

"This is serious, Cousin Tabitha," said Ribby. "We must send for John Joiner at once, with a saw."

* * * * *

Now this is what had been happening to Tom Kitten, and it shows how very unwise it is to go up a chimney in a very old house, where a person does not know his way, and where there are enormous rats.

Tom Kitten did not want to be shut up in a cupboard. When he saw that his mother was going to bake, he determined to hide.

He looked about for a nice convenient place, and he fixed upon the chimney.

The fire had only just been lighted, and it was not hot; but there was a white choky smoke from the green sticks. Tom Kitten got upon the fender and looked up. It was a big old-fashioned fire-place.

The chimney itself was wide enough inside for a man to stand up and walk about. So there was plenty of room for a little Tom Cat.

He jumped right up into the fire-place, balancing himself upon the iron bar where the kettle hangs.

Tom Kitten took another big jump off the bar, and landed on a ledge high up inside the chimney, knocking down some soot into the fender.

Tom Kitten coughed and choked with the smoke; and he could hear the sticks beginning to crackle and burn in the fire-place down below. He made up his mind to climb right to the top, and get out on the slates, and try to catch sparrows.

"I cannot go back. If I slipped I might fall in the fire and singe my beautiful tail and my little blue jacket."

The chimney was a very big old-fashioned one. It was built in the days when people burnt logs of wood upon the hearth.

The chimney stack stood up above the roof like a little stone tower, and the daylight shone down from the top, under the slanting slates that kept out the rain.

Tom Kitten was getting very frightened! He climbed up, and up, and up.

Then he waded sideways through inches of soot. He was like a little sweep himself.

It was most confusing in the dark. One flue seemed to lead into another.

There was less smoke, but Tom Kitten felt quite lost.

He scrambled up and up; but before he reached the chimney top he came to a place where somebody had loosened a stone in the wall. There were some mutton bones lying about—

"This seems funny," said Tom Kitten. "Who has been gnawing bones up here in the chimney? I wish I had never come! And what a funny smell? It is something like mouse; only dreadfully strong. It makes me sneeze," said Tom Kitten.

He squeezed through the hole in the wall, and dragged himself along a most uncomfortably tight passage where there was scarcely any light.

He groped his way carefully for several yards; he was at the back of the skirting-board in the attic, where there is a little mark * in the picture.

All at once he fell head over heels in the dark, down a hole, and landed on a heap of very dirty rags.

When Tom Kitten picked himself up and looked about him— he found himself in a place that he had never seen before,

although he had lived all his life in the house.

It was a very small stuffy fusty room, with boards, and rafters, and cobwebs, and lath and plaster.

Opposite to him—as far away as he could sit—was an enormous rat.

"What do you mean by tumbling into my

bed all covered with smuts?" said the rat, chattering his teeth.

"Please sir, the chimney wants sweeping," said poor Tom Kitten.

"Anna Maria! Anna Maria!" squeaked the rat. There was a pattering noise and an old woman rat poked her head round a rafter.

All in a minute she rushed upon Tom Kitten, and before he knew what was happening—

His coat was pulled off, and he was rolled up in a bundle, and tied with string in very hard knots.

Anna Maria did the tying. The old rat watched her and took snuff. When she had finished, they both sat staring at him with their mouths open.

"Anna Maria," said the old man rat (whose name was Samuel Whiskers), "Anna Maria, make me a kitten dumpling roly-poly pudding for my dinner."

"It requires dough and a pat of butter, and a rolling-pin,' said Anna Maria, considering Tom Kitten with her head on one side.

"No," said Samuel Whiskers, "make it properly, Anna Maria, with breadcrumbs."

"Nonsense! Butter and dough," replied Anna Maria.

The two rats consulted together for a few minutes and then went away.

Samuel Whiskers got through a hole in the wainscot, and went boldly down the front staircase to the dairy to get the butter. He did not meet anybody.

He made a second journey for the rolling-pin. He pushed it in front of him with his paws, like a brewer's man trundling a barrel.

He could hear Ribby and Tabitha talking, but they were busy lighting the candle to look into the chest. They did not see him.

Anna Maria went down by way of the skirting-board and a window shutter to the kitchen to steal the dough.

She borrowed a small saucer, and scooped up the dough with her paws.

She did not observe Moppet.

While Tom Kitten was left alone under the floor of the attic, he wriggled about and tried to mew for help.

But his mouth was full of soot and cobwebs, and he was tied up in such very tight knots, he could not make anybody hear him.

Except a spider, which came out of a crack in the ceiling and examined the knots critically, from a safe distance.

It was a judge of knots because it had a habit of tying up unfortunate blue-bottles. It did not offer to assist him.

Tom Kitten wriggled and squirmed until he was quite exhausted.

Presently the rats came back and set to work to make him into a dumpling. First they smeared him with butter, and then they rolled him in the dough.

"Will not the string be very indigestible, Anna Maria?" inquired Samuel Whiskers.

Anna Maria said she thought that it was of no consequence; but she wished that Tom Kitten would hold his head still, as it disarranged the pastry.
She laid hold of his ears.

Tom Kitten bit and spat, and mewed and wriggled; and the rolling-pin went roly-poly, roly; roly, poly, roly. The rats each held an end.

"His tail is sticking out! You did not fetch enough dough, Anna Maria."

"I fetched as much as I could carry," replied Anna Maria.

"I do not think"— said Samuel Whiskers, pausing to take a look at Tom Kitten—"I do *not* think it will be a good pudding. It smells sooty."

Anna Maria was about to argue the

point, when all at once there began to be other sounds up above—the rasping noise of a saw; and the noise of a little dog, scratching and yelping!

The rats dropped the rolling-pin, and listened attentively.

"We are discovered and interrupted, Anna Maria; let us collect our property—and other people's,—and depart at once."

"I fear that we shall be obliged to leave this pudding."

"But I am persuaded that the knots would have proved indigestible, whatever you may urge to the contrary."

"Come away at once and help me to tie up some mutton bones in a counterpane," said Anna Maria. "I have got half a smoked ham hidden in the chimney."

So it happened that by the time John Joiner had got the plank up—there was nobody under the floor except the rolling-pin and Tom Kitten in a very dirty dumpling!

But there was a strong smell of rats; and John Joiner spent the rest of the morning sniffing and whining, and wagging his tail, and going round and round with his head in the hole like a gimlet.

Then he nailed the plank down again and put his tools in his bag, and came downstairs.

The cat family had quite recovered. They invited him to stay to dinner.

The dumpling had been peeled off Tom Kitten, and made separately into a bag pudding, with currants in it to hide the smuts.

They had been obliged to put Tom Kitten into a hot bath to get the butter off.

John Joiner smelt the pudding; but he regretted that he had not time to stay to dinner, because he had just finished making a wheel-barrow for Miss Potter, and she had ordered two hen-coops.

And when I was going to the post late in the afternoon—I looked up the lane from the corner, and I saw Mr. Samuel Whiskers and his wife on the run, with big bundles on a little wheel-barrow, which looked very like mine.

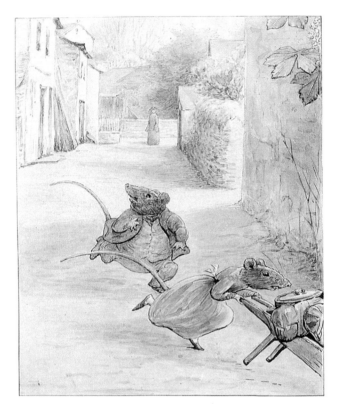

They were just turning in at the gate to the barn of Farmer Potatoes.

Samuel Whiskers was puffing and out of breath. Anna Maria was still arguing in shrill tones.

She seemed to know her way, and she seemed to have a quantity of luggage.

I am sure *I* never gave her leave to borrow my wheel-barrow!

They went into the barn, and hauled their parcels with a bit of string to the top of the hay mow.

After that, there were no
more rats for a long time at
Tabitha Twitchit's.

As for Farmer Potatoes,
he has been driven nearly
distracted. There are rats,
and rats, and rats in his
barn! They eat up the
chicken food, and steal the
oats and bran, and make holes
in the meal bags.

And they are all
descended from Mr.
and Mrs. Samuel
Whiskers—children
and grand-children
and great great grand-
children.

There is no end to
them!

Moppet and Mittens have grown up into very good rat-catchers.

They go out rat-catching in the village, and they find plenty of employment. They charge so much a dozen, and earn their living very comfortably.

They hang up the rats' tails in a row on the barn door, to show how many they have caught—dozens and dozens of them.

But Tom Kitten has always been afraid of a rat; he never durst face anything that is bigger than—

A Mouse.

THE END

THE TALE OF
THE
FLOPSY BUNNIES

1909

ABOUT THIS BOOK

The Tale of The Flopsy Bunnies pays another visit to the world of Peter Rabbit and Benjamin Bunny. Both rabbits have now grown up, Benjamin has married Peter's sister Flopsy and although still "improvident and cheerful", has a large family to care for. Beatrix Potter was well aware that her earlier books had created a huge demand for rabbit stories, and dedicated this one, "For all little friends of Mr. McGregor and Peter and Benjamin." Besides, she enjoyed painting rabbits, and gardens too. When preparing the book in 1909 she was staying with her uncle Fred and aunt Harriet Burton at Gwaynynog, their large house in Wales, and made many studies of the garden there. She described it on an earlier visit as "the prettiest kind of garden, where bright old-fashioned flowers grow amongst the currant bushes." It is beautifully depicted in her lovely illustrations.

IT is said that the effect of eating too much lettuce is "soporific".

I have never felt sleepy after eating lettuces; but then *I* am not a rabbit.

They certainly had a very soporific effect upon the Flopsy Bunnies!

When Benjamin Bunny grew up, he married his Cousin Flopsy. They had a large family, and they were very improvident and cheerful.

I do not remember the separate names of their children; they were generally called the "Flopsy Bunnies".

As there was not always quite enough to eat—Benjamin used to borrow cabbages from Flopsy's brother, Peter Rabbit, who kept a nursery garden.

Sometimes Peter Rabbit had no cabbages to spare.

When this happened, the Flopsy Bunnies went across the field to a rubbish heap, in the ditch outside Mr. McGregor's garden.

Mr. McGregor's rubbish heap was a mixture. There were jam pots and paper bags, and mountains of chopped grass from the mowing machine (which always tasted oily), and some rotten vegetable marrows and an old boot or two. One day—oh joy!—there were a quantity of overgrown lettuces, which had "shot" into flower.

The Flopsy Bunnies simply stuffed lettuces. By degrees, one after another, they were overcome with slumber, and lay down in the mown grass.

Benjamin was not so much overcome as his children. Before going to sleep he was sufficiently wide awake to put a paper bag over his head to keep off the flies.

The little Flopsy Bunnies slept delightfully in the warm sun. From the lawn beyond the garden came the distant clacketty sound of the mowing machine. The blue-bottles buzzed about the wall, and a little old mouse picked over the rubbish among the jam pots.

(I can tell you her name, she was called Thomasina Tittlemouse, a woodmouse with a long tail.)

She rustled across the paper bag, and awakened Benjamin Bunny.

The mouse apologized profusely, and said that she knew Peter Rabbit.

While she and Benjamin were talking, close under the wall, they heard a heavy tread above their heads; and suddenly Mr. McGregor emptied out a sackful of lawn mowings right upon the top of the sleeping Flopsy Bunnies! Benjamin shrank down under his paper bag. The mouse hid in a jam pot.

The little rabbits smiled sweetly in their sleep under the shower of grass; they did not awake because the lettuces had been so soporific.

They dreamt that their mother Flopsy was tucking them up in a hay bed.

Mr. McGregor looked down after emptying his sack. He saw some funny little brown tips of ears sticking up through the lawn mowings. He stared at them for some time.

Presently a fly settled on one of them and it moved.

Mr. McGregor climbed down on to the rubbish heap—

"One, two, three, four! five! six leetle rabbits!" said he as he dropped them into his sack.

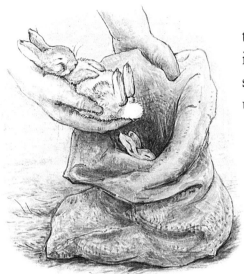

The Flopsy Bunnies dreamt that their mother was turning them over in bed. They stirred a little in their sleep, but still they did not wake up.

Mr. McGregor tied up the sack and left it on the wall.

He went to put away the mowing machine.

While he was gone, Mrs. Flopsy Bunny (who had remained at home) came across the field.

She looked suspiciously at the sack and wondered where everybody was?

Then the mouse came out of her jam pot, and Benjamin took the paper bag off his head, and they told the doleful tale.

Benjamin and Flopsy were in despair, they could not undo the string.

But Mrs. Tittlemouse was a resourceful person. She nibbled a hole in the bottom corner of the sack.

The little rabbits were pulled out and pinched to wake them.

Their parents stuffed the empty sack with three rotten vegetable marrows, an old blacking-brush and two decayed turnips.

Then they all hid under a bush and watched for Mr. McGregor.

Mr. McGregor came back and picked up the sack, and carried it off.

He carried it hanging down, as if it were rather heavy.

The Flopsy Bunnies followed at a safe distance.

They watched him go into his house.

And then they crept up to the window to listen.

Mr. McGregor threw down the sack on the stone floor in a way that would have been extremely painful to the Flopsy Bunnies, if they had happened to have been inside it.

They could hear him drag his chair on the flags, and chuckle—

"One, two, three, four, five, six leetle rabbits!" said Mr. McGregor.

"Eh? What's that? What have they been spoiling now?" inquired Mrs. McGregor.

"One, two, three, four, five, six leetle fat rabbits!" repeated Mr. McGregor, counting on his fingers—"one, two, three—"

"Don't you be silly; what do you mean, you silly old man?"

"In the sack! One, two, three, four, five, six!" replied Mr. McGregor.

(The youngest Flopsy Bunny got upon the window-sill.)

Mrs. McGregor took hold of the sack and felt it. She said she could feel six, but they must be *old* rabbits, because they were so hard and all different shapes.

"Not fit to eat; but the skins will do fine to line my old cloak."

"Line your old cloak?" shouted Mr. McGregor—"I shall sell them and buy myself baccy!"

"Rabbit tobacco! I shall skin them and cut off their heads."

Mrs. McGregor untied the sack and put her hand inside.

When she felt the vegetables she became very very angry. She said that Mr. McGregor had "done it a purpose".

And Mr. McGregor was very angry too. One of the rotten marrows came flying through the kitchen window, and hit the youngest Flopsy Bunny.

It was rather hurt.

Then Benjamin and Flopsy thought that it was time to go home.

So Mr. McGregor did not get his tobacco, and Mrs. McGregor did not get her rabbit skins.

But next Christmas Thomasina Tittlemouse got a present of enough rabbit-wool to make herself a cloak and a hood, and a handsome muff and a pair of warm mittens.

THE END

THE TALE OF GINGER AND PICKLES

1909

ABOUT THIS BOOK

The Tale of Ginger and Pickles caused much amusement among the villagers of Sawrey when it was published. "It has got a good many views which can be recognized in the village which is what they like," Beatrix wrote to Milly Warne, Harold and Norman's sister. The story also features some familiar friends from previous books, going about their everyday business. Even the policeman from *The Tale of Two Bad Mice* makes an appearance, as do the dolls, Lucinda and Jane.

The book is dedicated to John Taylor, whose wife kept the village shop in Sawrey on which the story-book shop is based. Beatrix had said she couldn't put him in a story as he was always in bed, which explains her dedication, "With very kind regards to old Mr. John Taylor, who 'thinks he might pass as a dormouse!' (Three years in bed and never a grumble!)"

ONCE upon a time there was a village shop. The name over the window was "Ginger and Pickles".

It was a little small shop just the right size for Dolls— Lucinda and Jane Doll-cook always bought their groceries at Ginger and Pickles.

The counter inside was a convenient height for rabbits. Ginger and Pickles sold red spotty pocket-handkerchiefs at a penny three farthings.

They also sold sugar, and snuff and goloshes.

In fact, although it was such a small shop it sold nearly everything—except a few things that you want in a hurry—like bootlaces, hair-pins and mutton chops.

Ginger and Pickles were the people who kept the shop. Ginger was a yellow tom-cat, and Pickles was a terrier.

The rabbits were always a little bit afraid of Pickles.

The shop was also patronized by mice—only the mice were rather afraid of Ginger.

Ginger usually requested Pickles to serve them, because he said it made his mouth water.

"I cannot bear," said he, "to see them going out at the door carrying their little parcels."

"I have the same feeling about rats," replied Pickles, "but it would never do to eat our own customers; they would leave us and go to Tabitha Twitchit's."

"On the contrary, they would go nowhere," replied Ginger gloomily.

(Tabitha Twitchit kept the only other shop in the village. She did not give credit.)

Ginger and Pickles gave unlimited credit.

Now the meaning of "credit" is this—when a customer buys a bar of soap, instead of the customer pulling out a purse and paying for it—she says she will pay another time.

And Pickles makes a low bow and says, "With pleasure, madam," and it is written down in a book.

The customers come again and again, and buy quantities, in spite of being afraid of Ginger and Pickles.

But there is no money in what is called the "till".

The customers came in crowds every day and bought quantities, especially the toffee customers. But there was always no money; they never paid for as much as a pennyworth of peppermints.

But the sales were enormous, ten times as large as Tabitha Twitchit's.

As there was always no money, Ginger and Pickles were obliged to eat their own goods.

Pickles ate biscuits and Ginger ate a dried haddock.

They ate them by candle-light after the shop was closed.

When it came to Jan. 1st there was still no money, and Pickles was unable to buy a dog licence.

"It is very unpleasant, I am afraid of the police," said Pickles.

"It is your own fault for being a terrier; *I* do not require a licence, and neither does Kep, the Collie dog."

"It is very uncomfortable, I am afraid I shall be summoned. I have tried in vain to get a licence upon credit at the Post Office;" said Pickles. "The place is full of policemen. I met one as I was coming home."

"Let us send in the bill again to Samuel Whiskers, Ginger, he owes 22/9 for bacon."

"I do not believe that he intends to pay at all," replied Ginger.

"And I feel sure that Anna Maria pockets things—Where are all the cream crackers?"

"You have eaten them yourself," replied Ginger.

Ginger and Pickles retired into the back parlour.

They did accounts. They added up sums and sums, and sums.

"Samuel Whiskers has run up a bill as long as his tail; he has had an ounce and three-quarters of snuff since October."

"What is seven pounds of butter at 1/3, and a stick of sealing wax and four matches?"

"Send in all the bills again to everybody 'with comp^{ts}'," replied Ginger.

After a time they heard a noise in the shop, as if something had been pushed in at the door. They came out of the back parlour. There was an envelope lying on the counter, and a policeman writing in a notebook!

Pickles nearly had a fit, he barked and he barked and made little rushes.

"Bite him, Pickles! bite him!" spluttered Ginger behind a sugar-barrel, "he's only a German doll!"

The policeman went on writing in his note-book; twice he put his pencil in his mouth, and once he dipped it in the treacle.

Pickles barked till he was hoarse. But still the policeman took no notice. He had bead eyes, and his helmet was sewed on with stitches.

At length on his last little rush—Pickles found that the shop was empty. The policeman had disappeared.

But the envelope remained. "Do you think that he has gone to fetch a real live policeman? I am afraid it is a summons," said Pickles.

"No," replied Ginger, who had opened the envelope, "it is the rates and taxes, £3 19 11¾."

"This is the last straw," said Pickles, "let us close the shop."

They put up the shutters, and left. But they have not removed from the neighbourhood. In fact some people wish they had gone further.

Ginger is living in the warren. I do not know what occupation he pursues; he looks stout and comfortable.

Pickles is at present a gamekeeper.

The closing of the shop caused great inconvenience. Tabitha Twitchit immediately raised the price of everything a half-penny; and she continued to refuse to give credit.

Of course there are the tradesmen's carts—the butcher, the fish-man and Timothy Baker.

But a person cannot live on "seed wigs" and sponge-cake and butter-buns—not even when the sponge-cake is as good as Timothy's!

After a time Mr. John Dormouse and his daughter began to sell peppermints and candles.

But they did not keep "self-fitting sixes"; and it takes five mice to carry one seven inch candle.

Besides—the candles
which they sell behave
very strangely in warm
weather.

And Miss Dormouse
refused to take back the
ends when they were
brought back to her with complaints.

And when Mr. John
Dormouse was complained
to, he stayed in bed, and
would say nothing but
"very snug"; which is not
the way to carry on a retail
business.

So everybody was pleased
when Sally Henny Penny sent
out a printed poster to say that
she was going to re-open the
shop—"Henny's Opening Sale!
Grand co-operative Jumble!
Penny's penny prices! Come buy,
come try, come buy!"

The poster really was most 'ticing.

There was a rush upon the opening day. The shop was crammed with customers, and there were crowds of mice upon the biscuit canisters.

Sally Henny Penny gets rather flustered when she tries to count out change, and she insists on being paid cash; but she is quite harmless.

And she has laid in a remarkable assortment of bargains. There is something to please everybody.

THE END

THE TALE OF
MRS. TITTLEMOUSE

1910

About This Book

Beatrix Potter's interest in all kinds of creatures, from spiders to bees, is clearly evident in *The Tale of Mrs. Tittlemouse*. There are no people in the story, but all sorts of creepy-crawly characters invade Mrs. Tittlemouse's tidy home. Originally, Beatrix had woodlice, an earwig and a centipede among the uninvited guests, but her publishers felt the first two insects were unsuitable for a children's book! Beatrix herself decided against the centipede, replacing it with a most beautiful picture of Miss Butterfly tasting the sugar. She evidently bore no grudge against her editor for the alterations he requested, for the book is dedicated to Harold Warne's daughter Nellie, who also received the manuscript as a New Year's present.

ONCE upon a time there was a wood-mouse, and her name was Mrs. Tittlemouse.

She lived in a bank under a hedge.

Such a funny house!

There were yards and yards of sandy passages, leading to storerooms and nut-cellars and seed-cellars, all amongst the roots of the hedge.

There was a kitchen, a parlour, a pantry, and a larder.

Also, there was Mrs. Tittlemouse's bedroom, where she slept in a little box bed!

Mrs. Tittlemouse was a most terribly tidy particular little mouse, always sweeping and dusting the soft sandy floors.

Sometimes a beetle lost its way in the passages.

"Shuh! shuh! little dirty feet!" said Mrs. Tittlemouse, clattering her dust-pan.

And one day a little old woman ran up and down in a red spotty cloak.

"Your house is on fire, Mother Ladybird! Fly away home to your children!"

Another day, a big fat spider came in to shelter from the rain.

"Beg pardon, is this not Miss Muffet's?"

"Go away, you bold bad spider! Leaving ends of cobweb all over my nice clean house!"

She bundled the spider out at a window.

He let himself down the hedge with a long thin bit of string.

Mrs. Tittlemouse went on her way to a distant storeroom, to fetch cherry-stones and thistle-down seed for dinner.

All along the passage she sniffed, and looked at the floor.

"I smell a smell of honey; is it the cowslips outside, in the hedge?

I am sure I can see the marks of little dirty feet."

Suddenly round a corner, she met Babbitty Bumble—"Zizz, Bizz, Bizzz!" said the bumble bee.

Mrs. Tittlemouse looked at her severely. She wished that she had a broom.

"Good-day, Babbitty Bumble; I should be glad to buy some beeswax. But what are you doing down here?

Why do you always come in at a window, and say 'Zizz, Bizz, Bizzz'?" Mrs. Tittlemouse began to get cross.

"Zizz, Wizz, Wizzz!" replied Babbitty Bumble in a peevish squeak. She sidled down a passage, and disappeared into a storeroom which had been used for acorns.

Mrs. Tittlemouse had eaten the acorns before Christmas; the storeroom ought to have been empty.

But it was full of untidy dry moss.

Mrs. Tittlemouse began to pull out the moss. Three or four other bees put their heads out, and buzzed fiercely.

"I am not in the habit of letting lodgings; this is an intrusion!" said Mrs. Tittlemouse. "I will have them turned out—"

"Buzz! Buzz! Buzzz!"

—"I wonder who would help me?"

"Bizz, Wizz, Wizzz!"

—"I will not have Mr. Jackson; he never wipes his feet."

Mrs. Tittlemouse decided to leave the bees till after dinner.

When she got back to the parlour, she heard someone coughing in a fat voice; and there sat Mr. Jackson himself!

He was sitting all over a small rocking-chair, twiddling his thumbs and smiling, with his feet on the fender.

He lived in a drain below the hedge, in a very dirty wet ditch.

"How do you do, Mr. Jackson? Deary me, you have got very wet!"

"Thank you, thank you, thank you, Mrs. Tittlemouse! I'll sit awhile and dry myself," said Mr. Jackson.

He sat and smiled, and the water dripped off his coat tails. Mrs. Tittlemouse went round with a mop.

He sat such a while that he had to be asked if he would take some dinner?

First she offered him cherry-stones. "Thank you, thank you, Mrs. Tittlemouse! No teeth, no teeth, no teeth!" said Mr. Jackson.

He opened his mouth most unnecessarily wide; he certainly had not a tooth in his head.

Then she offered him thistle-down seed—"Tiddly, widdly, widdly! Pouff, pouff, puff!" said Mr. Jackson. He blew the thistle-down all over the room.

"Thank you, thank you, thank you, Mrs. Tittlemouse! Now what I really—*really* should like —would be a little dish of honey!"

"I am afraid I have not got any, Mr. Jackson," said Mrs. Tittlemouse.

"Tiddly, widdly, widdly, Mrs. Tittlemouse!" said the smiling Mr. Jackson, "I can *smell* it; that is why I came to call."

Mr. Jackson rose ponderously from the table, and began to look into the cupboards.

Mrs. Tittlemouse followed him with a dish-cloth, to wipe his large wet footmarks off the parlour floor.

When he had convinced himself that there was no honey in the cupboards, he began to walk down the passage.

"Indeed, indeed, you will stick fast, Mr. Jackson!"

"Tiddly, widdly, widdly, Mrs. Tittlemouse!"

First he squeezed into the pantry.

"Tiddly, widdly, widdly? No honey? No honey, Mrs. Tittlemouse?"

There were three creepy-crawly people hiding in the plate-rack. Two of them got away; but the littlest one he caught.

Then he squeezed into the larder. Miss Butterfly was tasting the sugar; but she flew away out of the window.

"Tiddly, widdly, widdly, Mrs. Tittlemouse; you seem to have plenty of visitors!"

"And without any invitation!" said Mrs. Thomasina Tittlemouse.

They went along the sandy passage—"Tiddly widdly—" "Buzz! Wizz! Wizz!"

He met Babbitty round a corner, and snapped her up, and put her down again.

"I do not like bumble bees. They are all over bristles," said Mr. Jackson, wiping his mouth with his coat-sleeve.

"Get out, you nasty old toad!" shrieked Babbitty Bumble.

"I shall go distracted!" scolded Mrs. Tittlemouse.

She shut herself up in the nut-cellar while Mr. Jackson pulled out the bees-nest. He seemed to have no objection to stings.

When Mrs. Tittlemouse ventured to come out—everybody had gone away.

But the untidiness was something dreadful—"Never did I see such a mess—smears of honey; and moss, and thistle-down—and marks of big and little dirty feet—all over my nice clean house!"

She gathered up the moss and the remains of the beeswax.

Then she went out and fetched some twigs, to partly close up the front door.

"I will make it too small for Mr. Jackson!"

She fetched soft soap, and flannel, and a new scrubbing brush from the storeroom. But she was too tired to do any more.

First she fell asleep in her chair, and then she went to bed.

"Will it ever be tidy again?" said poor Mrs. Tittlemouse.

Next morning she got up very early and began a spring cleaning which lasted a fortnight.

She swept, and scrubbed, and dusted; and she rubbed up the furniture with beeswax, and polished her little tin spoons.

When it was all beautifully neat and clean, she gave a party to five other little mice, without Mr. Jackson.

He smelt the party and came up the bank, but he could not squeeze in at the door.

So they handed him out acorn-cupfuls of honey-dew through the window, and he was not at all offended.

He sat outside in the sun, and said—"Tiddly, widdly, widdly! Your very good health, Mrs. Tittlemouse!"

THE END

THE TALE OF
TIMMY TIPTOES

1911

ABOUT THIS BOOK

As Beatrix Potter's books continued to sell, she became known in America as well as Britain, receiving letters from eager readers far and wide. *The Tale of Timmy Tiptoes* was written to appeal to an American audience, with grey squirrels (which originally came to Britain from America), chipmunks and a black bear. Even the book's dedication shows the author departing from her usual very personal message to look further afield: "For many unknown little friends, including Monica." Monica was "the school friend of a little cousin, who asked for it as a favour, and the name took my fancy," as Beatrix explained later. By this time (1911), she was very occupied with farming and looking after her elderly parents, and Timmy Tiptoes' story was the only book to appear in that year.

ONCE upon a time there was a little fat comfortable grey squirrel, called Timmy Tiptoes. He had a nest thatched with leaves in the top of a tall tree; and he had a little squirrel wife called Goody.

Timmy Tiptoes sat out, enjoying the breeze; he whisked his tail and chuckled—"Little wife Goody, the nuts are ripe; we must lay up a store for winter and spring."

Goody Tiptoes was busy pushing moss under the thatch —"The nest is so snug, we shall be sound asleep all winter."

"Then we shall wake up all the thinner, when there is nothing to eat in spring-time," replied prudent Timothy.

When Timmy and Goody Tiptoes came to the nut thicket, they found other squirrels were there already.

Timmy took off his jacket and hung it on a twig; they worked away quietly by themselves.

Every day they made several journeys and picked quantities of nuts. They carried them away in bags, and stored them in several hollow stumps near the tree where they had built their nest.

When these stumps were full, they began to empty the bags into a hole high up a tree, that had belonged to a wood-pecker; the nuts rattled down—down —down inside.

"How shall you ever get them out again? It is like a money-box!" said Goody.

"I shall be much thinner before spring-time, my love," said Timmy Tiptoes, peeping into the hole.

They did collect quantities —because they did not lose them!

Squirrels who bury their nuts in the ground lose more than half, because they cannot remember the place.

The most forgetful squirrel in the wood was called Silver-tail. He began to dig, and he could not remember. And then he dug again and found some nuts that did not belong to him; and there was a fight. And the other squirrels began to dig—the whole wood was in commotion!

Unfortunately, just at this time a flock of little birds flew by, from bush to bush, searching for green caterpillars and spiders. There were several sorts of little birds, twittering different songs.

The first one sang—"Who's bin digging-up *my* nuts? Who's-been-digging-up *my* nuts?"

And another sang—"Little bit-a-bread and-*no*-cheese! Little bit-a-bread an'-*no*-cheese!"

The squirrels followed and listened. The first little bird flew into the bush where Timmy and Goody Tiptoes were quietly tying up their bags, and it sang—"Who's-bin digging-up *my* nuts? Who's been digging-up *my*-nuts?"

Timmy Tiptoes went on with his work without replying; indeed, the little bird did not expect an answer. It was only singing its natural song, and it meant nothing at all.

But when the other squirrels heard that song, they rushed upon Timmy Tiptoes and cuffed and scratched him, and upset his bag of nuts. The innocent little bird which had caused all the mischief, flew away in a fright!

Timmy rolled over and over, and then turned tail and fled towards his nest, followed by a crowd of squirrels shouting—"Who's-been digging-up *my*-nuts?"

They caught him and dragged him up the very same tree, where there was the little round hole, and they pushed him in. The hole was much too small for Timmy Tiptoes' figure. They squeezed him dreadfully, it was a wonder they did not break his ribs. "We will leave him here till he confesses," said Silvertail Squirrel, and he shouted into the hole— "Who's-been-digging-up *my*-nuts?"

Timmy Tiptoes made no reply; he had tumbled down inside the tree, upon half a peck of nuts belonging to himself. He lay quite stunned and still.

Goody Tiptoes picked up the nut bags and went home. She made a cup of tea for Timmy; but he didn't come and didn't come.

Goody Tiptoes passed a lonely and unhappy night. Next morning she ventured back to the nut-bushes to look for him; but the other unkind squirrels drove her away.

She wandered all over the wood, calling—

"Timmy Tiptoes! Timmy Tiptoes! Oh, where is Timmy Tiptoes?"

In the meantime Timmy Tiptoes came to his senses. He found himself tucked up in a little moss bed, very much in the dark, feeling sore; it seemed to be under ground. Timmy coughed and groaned, because his ribs hurted him. There was a chirpy noise, and a small striped Chipmunk appeared with a night light, and hoped he felt better?

It was most kind to Timmy Tiptoes; it lent him its night-cap; and the house was full of provisions.

The Chipmunk explained that it had rained nuts through the top of the tree—"Besides, I found a few buried!" It laughed and chuckled when it heard Timmy's story. While Timmy was confined to bed, it 'ticed him to eat quantities— "But how shall I ever get out through that hole unless I thin myself? My wife will be anxious!" "Just another nut— or two nuts; let me crack them for you," said the Chipmunk. Timmy Tiptoes grew fatter and fatter!

Now Goody Tiptoes had set to work again by herself. She did not put any more nuts into the wood-pecker's hole, because she had always doubted how they could be got out again. She hid them under a tree root; they rattled down, down, down. Once when Goody emptied an extra big bagful, there was a decided squeak; and next time Goody brought another bagful, a little striped Chipmunk scrambled out in a hurry.

"It is getting perfectly full-up downstairs; the sitting-room is full, and they are rolling along the passage; and my husband, Chippy Hackee, has run away and left me. What is the explanation of these showers of nuts?"

"I am sure I beg your pardon; I did not know that anybody lived here," said Mrs. Goody Tiptoes; "but where is Chippy Hackee? My husband, Timmy Tiptoes, has run away too."

"I know where Chippy is; a little bird told me," said Mrs. Chippy Hackee.

She led the way to the wood-pecker's tree, and they listened at the hole.

Down below there was a noise of nut crackers, and a fat squirrel voice and a thin squirrel voice were singing together—

"My little old man and I fell out,
How shall we bring this matter
    about?
Bring it about as well as you can,
And get you gone, you little old
    man!"

"You could squeeze in, through that little round hole," said Goody Tiptoes.

"Yes, I could," said the Chipmunk, "but my husband, Chippy Hackee, bites!"

Down below there was a noise of cracking nuts and nibbling; and then the fat squirrel voice and the thin squirrel voice sang—

"For the diddlum day
Day diddle dum di!
Day diddle diddle dum day!"

Then Goody peeped in at the hole, and called down— "Timmy Tiptoes! Oh fie, Timmy Tiptoes!" And Timmy replied, "Is that you, Goody Tiptoes? Why, certainly!"

He came up and kissed Goody through the hole; but he was so fat that he could not get out.

Chippy Hackee was not too fat, but he did not want to come; he stayed down below and chuckled.

And so it went on for a fortnight; till a big wind blew off the top of the tree, and opened up the hole and let in the rain.

Then Timmy Tiptoes came out, and went home with an umbrella.

But Chippy Hackee continued to camp out for another week, although it was uncomfortable.

At last a large bear came walking through the wood. Perhaps he also was looking for nuts; he seemed to be sniffing around.

Chippy Hackee went home in a hurry!

And when Chippy Hackee got home, he found he had caught a cold in his head; and he was more uncomfortable still.

And now Timmy and Goody Tiptoes keep their nut-store fastened up with a little padlock.

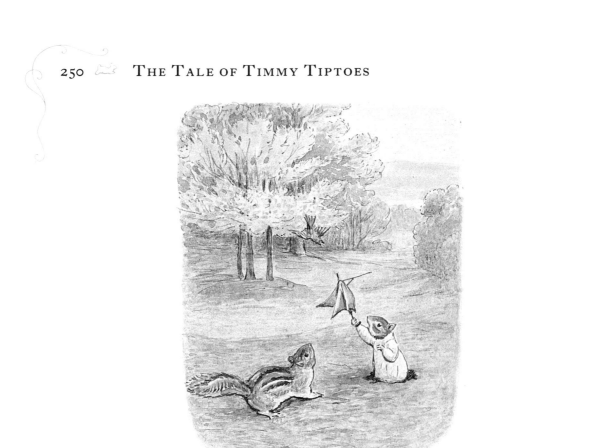

And whenever that little bird sees the Chipmunks, he sings—"Who's-been-digging-up *my*-nuts? Who's been digging-up *my*-nuts?"

But nobody ever answers!

THE END

THE TALE OF
MR. TOD

1912

About This Book

With the publication of this story Beatrix Potter claimed to be tired of writing "goody goody books about nice people". Her principal characters, Mr. Tod (the old Saxon name for a fox) and Tommy Brock (the country word for a badger), are indeed disagreeable, though their story has a happy ending. There are not many colour pictures in the book, for Beatrix had less time for painting. Instead, she included many black-and-white illustrations in the style of woodcuts. The tale is set in Sawrey; Bull Banks, where Mr. Tod had his winter earth, was a pasture on Castle Farm, and Esthwaite Water can also be seen in some of the pictures. *Mr. Tod* was dedicated to "Francis William of Ulva – someday!" He was the baby son of Beatrix's cousin, Caroline Hutton, who had married the Laird of Ulva.

I have made many books about well-behaved people. Now, for a change, I am going to make a story about two disagreeable people, called Tommy Brock and Mr. Tod.

Nobody could call Mr. Tod "nice". The rabbits could not bear him; they could smell him half a mile off. He was of a wandering habit and he had foxey whiskers; they never knew where he would be next.

One day he was living in a stick-house in the coppice, causing terror to the family of old Mr. Benjamin Bouncer. Next day he moved into a pollard willow near the lake, frightening the wild ducks and the water rats.

In winter and early spring he might generally be found in an earth amongst the rocks at the top of Bull Banks, under Oatmeal Crag.

He had half a dozen houses, but he was seldom at home.

The houses were not always empty when Mr. Tod moved *out*; because sometimes Tommy Brock moved *in;* (without asking leave).

Tommy Brock was a short bristly fat waddling person with a grin; he grinned all over his face. He was not nice in his habits.

He ate wasp nests and frogs and worms; and he waddled about by moon-light, digging things up.

253

His clothes were very dirty; and as he slept in the day-time, he always went to bed in his boots. And the bed which he went to bed in, was generally Mr. Tod's.

Now Tommy Brock did occasionally eat rabbit-pie; but it was only very little young ones occasionally, when other food was really scarce. He was friendly with old Mr. Bouncer; they agreed in disliking the wicked otters and Mr. Tod; they often talked over that painful subject.

Old Mr. Bouncer was stricken in years. He sat in the spring

sunshine outside the burrow, in a muffler; smoking a pipe of rabbit tobacco.

He lived with his son Benjamin Bunny and his daughter-in-law Flopsy, who had a young family. Old Mr. Bouncer was in charge of the family that afternoon, because Benjamin and Flopsy had gone out.

The little rabbit-babies were just old enough to open their blue eyes and kick. They lay in a fluffy bed of rabbit wool and hay, in a shallow burrow, separate from the main rabbit hole. To tell the truth—old Mr. Bouncer had forgotten them.

He sat in the sun, and conversed cordially with Tommy Brock, who was passing through the wood with a sack and a little spud which he used for digging, and some mole traps. He complained bitterly about the scarcity of pheasants' eggs, and accused Mr. Tod of poaching them. And the otters had cleared

off all the frogs while he was asleep in winter—"I have not had a good square meal for a fortnight, I am living on pig-nuts. I shall have to turn vegetarian and eat my own tail!" said Tommy Brock.

It was not much of a joke, but it tickled old Mr. Bouncer; because Tommy Brock was so fat and stumpy and grinning.

So old Mr. Bouncer laughed; and pressed Tommy Brock to come inside, to taste a slice of seed-cake and "a glass of my daughter Flopsy's cowslip wine". Tommy Brock squeezed himself into the rabbit hole with alacrity.

Then old Mr. Bouncer smoked another pipe, and gave Tommy Brock a cabbage leaf cigar which was so very strong that it made Tommy Brock grin more than ever; and the smoke filled the burrow. Old Mr. Bouncer coughed and laughed; and Tommy Brock puffed and grinned.

And Mr. Bouncer laughed and coughed, and shut his eyes because of the cabbage smoke . . .

When Flopsy and Benjamin came back—old Mr. Bouncer woke up. Tommy Brock and all the young rabbit-babies had disappeared!

Mr. Bouncer would not confess that he had admitted anybody into the rabbit hole. But the smell of badger was undeniable; and there were round heavy footmarks in the sand. He was in disgrace; Flopsy wrung her ears, and slapped him.

Benjamin Bunny set off at once after Tommy Brock.

There was not much difficulty in tracking him; he had left his footmark and gone slowly up the winding footpath through the wood. Here he had rooted up the moss and wood sorrel. There he had dug quite a deep hole for dog darnel; and had set a mole trap. A little stream crossed the way. Benjamin skipped lightly over dry-foot; the badger's heavy steps showed plainly in the mud.

The path led to a part of the thicket where the trees had been cleared; there were leafy oak stumps, and a sea of blue hyacinths—but the smell that made Benjamin stop, was *not* the smell of flowers!

Mr. Tod's stick house was before him and, for once, Mr. Tod was at home. There was not only a foxey flavour in proof of it—there was smoke coming out of the broken pail that served as a chimney.

Benjamin Bunny sat up, staring; his whiskers twitched. Inside the stick house somebody dropped a plate, and said something. Benjamin stamped his foot, and bolted.

He never stopped till he came to the other side of the wood. Apparently Tommy Brock had turned the same way. Upon the top of the wall, there were again the marks of badger; and some ravellings of a sack had caught on a briar.

Benjamin climbed over the wall, into a meadow. He found another mole trap newly set; he was still upon the track of Tommy Brock. It was getting late in the afternoon. Other rabbits were coming out to enjoy the evening air. One of them in a blue coat by himself, was busily hunting for dandelions.— "Cousin Peter! Peter Rabbit, Peter Rabbit!" shouted Benjamin Bunny.

The blue-coated rabbit sat up with pricked ears—

"Whatever is the matter, Cousin Benjamin? Is it a cat? or John Stoat Ferret?"

"No, no, no! He's bagged my family—Tommy Brock—in a sack—have you seen him?"

"Tommy Brock? How many, Cousin Benjamin?"

"Seven, Cousin Peter, and all of them twins! Did he come this way? Please tell me quick!"

"Yes, yes; not ten minutes since . . . he said they were *caterpillars;* I did think they were kicking rather hard, for caterpillars."

"Which way? Which way has he gone, Cousin Peter?"

"He had a sack with something 'live in it; I watched him set a mole trap. Let me use my mind, Cousin Benjamin; tell me from the beginning." Benjamin did so.

"My Uncle Bouncer has displayed a lamentable want of discretion for his years;" said Peter reflectively, "but there are two hopeful circumstances. Your family is alive and kicking; and Tommy Brock has had refreshment. He will probably go to sleep, and keep them for breakfast."

"Which way?"

"Cousin Benjamin, compose yourself. I know very well which way. Because Mr. Tod was at home in the stick-house he has gone to Mr. Tod's other house, at the top of Bull Banks. I partly know, because he offered to leave any message at Sister Cottontail's; he said he would be passing." (Cottontail had married a black rabbit, and gone to live on the hill.)

Peter hid his dandelions, and accompanied the afflicted parent, who was all of a twitter. They crossed several fields and began to climb the hill; the tracks of Tommy Brock were plainly to be seen. He seemed to have put down the sack every dozen yards, to rest.

"He must be very puffed; we are close behind him, by the scent. What a nasty person!" said Peter.

The sunshine was still warm and slanting on the hill pastures. Half way up, Cottontail was sitting in her doorway, with four or five half-grown little rabbits playing about her; one black and the others brown.

Cottontail had seen Tommy Brock passing in the distance. Asked whether her husband was at home she replied that Tommy Brock had rested twice while she watched him.

He had nodded, and pointed to the sack, and seemed doubled up with laughing.—"Come away, Peter; he will be cooking them; come quicker!" said Benjamin Bunny.

They climbed up and up;—"He was at home; I saw his black ears peeping out of the hole." "They live too near the rocks to quarrel with their neighbours. Come on, Cousin Benjamin!"

When they came near the wood at the top of Bull Banks, they went cautiously. The trees grew amongst heaped-up rocks; and there, beneath a crag—Mr. Tod had made one of his homes. It was at the top of a steep bank; the rocks and bushes overhung it. The rabbits crept up carefully, listening and peeping.

This house was something between a cave, a prison, and a tumble-down pig-stye. There was a strong door, which was shut and locked.

The setting sun made the window panes glow like red flame; but the kitchen fire was not alight. It was neatly laid with dry sticks, as the rabbits could see, when they peeped through the window.

Benjamin sighed with relief.

But there were preparations upon the kitchen table which made him shudder. There was an immense empty pie-dish of

blue willow pattern, and a large carving knife and fork, and a chopper.

At the other end of the table was a partly unfolded tablecloth, a plate,

a tumbler, a knife and fork, salt-cellar, mustard and a chair —in short, preparations for one person's supper.

No person was to be seen, and no young rabbits. The kitchen was empty and silent; the clock had run down. Peter and Benjamin flattened their noses against the window, and stared into the dusk.

Then they scrambled round the rocks to the other side of the house. It was damp and smelly, and overgrown with thorns and briars.

The rabbits shivered in their shoes.

"Oh my poor rabbit babies! What a dreadful place; I shall never see them again!" sighed Benjamin.

They crept up to the bedroom window. It was closed and bolted like the kitchen. But there were signs that this window had been recently open; the cobwebs were disturbed, and there were fresh dirty footmarks upon the window-sill.

The room inside was so dark, that at first they could make out nothing; but they could hear a noise—a slow deep regular snoring grunt. And as their eyes became accustomed to the darkness, they perceived that somebody was asleep on Mr. Tod's bed, curled up under the blanket.—"He has gone to bed in his boots," whispered Peter.

Benjamin, who was all of a twitter, pulled Peter off the window-sill.

Tommy Brock's snores continued, grunty and regular from Mr. Tod's bed. Nothing could be seen of the young family.

The sun had set; an owl began to hoot in the wood. There were many unpleasant things lying about, that had much better have been buried; rabbit bones and skulls, and chickens' legs and other horrors. It was a shocking place, and very dark.

They went back to the front of the house, and tried in every way to move the bolt of the kitchen window. They tried to push up a rusty nail between the window sashes; but it was of no use, especially without a light.

They sat side by side outside the window, whispering and listening.

In half an hour the moon rose over the wood. It shone full and clear and cold, upon the house amongst the rocks, and in at the kitchen window.  But alas, no little rabbit babies were to be seen!

The moonbeams twinkled on the carving knife and the pie-dish, and made a path of brightness across the dirty floor.

The light showed a little door in a wall beside the kitchen fireplace—a little iron door belonging to a brick oven, of that old-fashioned sort that used to be heated with faggots of wood.

And presently at the same moment Peter and Benjamin noticed that whenever they shook the window—the little door opposite shook in answer. The young family were alive; shut up in the oven!

Benjamin was so excited that it was a mercy he did not awake Tommy Brock, whose snores continued solemnly in Mr. Tod's bed.

But there really was not very much comfort in the discovery. They could not open the window; and although the young family was alive—the little rabbits were quite incapable of letting themselves out; they were not old enough to crawl.

After much whispering, Peter and Benjamin decided to dig a tunnel. They began to burrow a yard or two lower down the bank. They hoped that they might be able to work between the large stones under the house; the kitchen floor was so dirty that it was impossible to say whether it was made of earth or flags.

They dug and dug for hours. They could not tunnel straight on account of stones; but by the end of the night they were under the kitchen floor. Benjamin was on his back, scratching upwards. Peter's claws were worn down; he was outside the tunnel, shuffling sand away. He called out that it was morning— sunrise; and that the jays were making a noise down below in the woods.

Benjamin Bunny came out of the dark tunnel, shaking the sand from his ears; he cleaned his face with his paws. Every minute the sun shone warmer on the top of the hill. In the valley there was a sea of white mist, with golden tops of trees showing through.

Again from the fields down below in the mist there came the angry cry of a jay—followed by the sharp yelping bark of a fox!

Then those two rabbits lost their heads completely. They did the most foolish thing that they could have done. They rushed into their short new tunnel, and hid themselves at the top end of it, under Mr. Tod's kitchen floor.

Mr. Tod was coming up Bull Banks, and he was in the very worst of tempers. First he had been upset by breaking the plate. It was his own fault; but it was a china plate, the last of the dinner service that had belonged to his grandmother, old Vixen Tod. Then the midges had been very bad. And he had

failed to catch a hen pheasant on her nest; and it had contained only five eggs, two of them addled. Mr. Tod had had an unsatisfactory night.

As usual, when out of humour, he determined to move house. First he tried the pollard willow, but it was damp; and the otters had left a dead fish near it. Mr. Tod likes nobody's leavings but his own.

He made his way up the hill; his temper was not improved by noticing unmistakable marks of badger. No one else grubs up the moss so wantonly as Tommy Brock.

Mr. Tod slapped his stick upon the earth and fumed; he guessed

where Tommy Brock had gone to. He
was further annoyed by the jay bird
which followed him persistently. It flew
from tree to tree and scolded, warning
every rabbit within hearing that either
a cat or a fox was coming up the
plantation. Once when it flew screaming

over his head—Mr. Tod snapped at it, and barked.

He approached his house very carefully, with a large rusty key.
He sniffed and his whiskers bristled. The house was locked up,
but Mr. Tod had his doubts whether it was empty. He turned
the rusty key in the lock; the rabbits below could hear it. Mr.
Tod opened the door cautiously and went in.

The sight that met Mr. Tod's eyes
in Mr. Tod's kitchen made Mr. Tod
furious. There was Mr. Tod's chair,
and Mr. Tod's pie-dish, and his
knife and fork and mustard and salt-
cellar and his tablecloth that he had
left folded up in the dresser—all set
out for supper (or breakfast)—
without doubt for that odious Tommy Brock.

There was a smell of fresh earth and dirty badger, which fortunately overpowered all smell of rabbit.

But what absorbed Mr. Tod's
attention was a noise—a deep slow
regular snoring grunting noise,
coming from his own bed.

He peeped through the hinges of
the half-open bedroom door. Then
he turned and came out of the house

in a hurry. His whiskers bristled and his coat-collar stood on end with rage.

For the next twenty minutes Mr. Tod kept creeping cautiously into the house, and retreating hurriedly out again. By degrees he ventured further in—right into the bedroom. When he was outside the house, he scratched up the earth with fury. But when he was inside—he did not like the look of Tommy Brock's teeth.

He was lying on his back with his mouth open, grinning from ear to ear. He snored peacefully and regularly; but one eye was not perfectly shut.

Mr Tod came in and out of the bedroom. Twice he brought in his walking-stick, and once he brought in the coal-scuttle. But he thought better of it, and took them away.

When he came back after removing the coal-scuttle, Tommy Brock was lying a little more sideways; but he seemed even sounder asleep. He was an incurably indolent person; he was not in the least afraid of Mr. Tod; he was simply too lazy and comfortable to move.

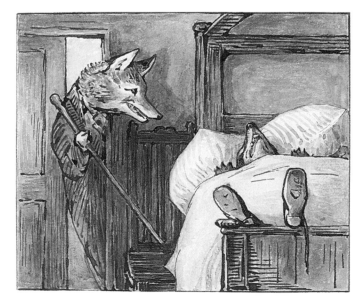

Mr. Tod came back yet again into the bedroom with a clothes line. He stood a minute watching Tommy Brock and listening attentively to the snores. They were very loud indeed, but seemed quite natural.

Mr. Tod turned his back towards the bed, and undid the window. It creaked; he turned round with a jump. Tommy Brock, who had opened one eye—shut it hastily. The snores continued.

Mr. Tod's proceedings were peculiar, and rather uneasy (because the bed was between the window and the door of the bedroom). He opened the

window a little way, and pushed out the greater part of the clothes line on to the window-sill. The rest of the line, with a hook at the end, remained in his hand.

Tommy Brock snored conscientiously. Mr. Tod stood and looked at him for a minute; then he left the room again.

Tommy Brock opened both eyes, and looked at the rope and grinned. There was a noise outside the window. Tommy Brock shut his eyes in a hurry.

Mr. Tod had gone out at the front door, and round to the back of the house. On the way, he stumbled over the rabbit

burrow. If he had had any idea who was inside it, he would have pulled them out quickly.

His foot went through the tunnel nearly upon the top of Peter Rabbit and Benjamin, but fortunately he thought that it was some more of Tommy Brock's work.

He took up the coil of line from the sill, listened for a moment, and then tied the rope to a tree.

Tommy Brock watched him with one eye, through the window. He was puzzled.

Mr. Tod fetched a large heavy pailful of water from the spring, and staggered with it through the kitchen into his bedroom.

Tommy Brock snored industriously, with rather a snort.

Mr. Tod put down the pail beside the bed, took up the end of rope with the hook—hesitated, and looked at Tommy Brock. The snores were almost apoplectic; but the grin was not quite so big.

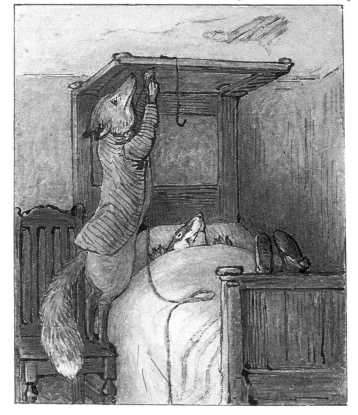

Mr. Tod gingerly mounted a chair by the head of the bedstead. His legs were dangerously near to Tommy Brock's teeth.

He reached up and put the end of rope, with the hook, over the head of the tester bed, where the curtains ought to hang.

(Mr. Tod's curtains were folded up, and put away, owing to the house being unoccupied. So was the counterpane. Tommy Brock was covered with a blanket only.) Mr. Tod standing on the unsteady chair looked down upon him attentively; he really was a first prize sound sleeper!

It seemed as though nothing would waken him—not even the flapping rope across the bed.

Mr. Tod descended safely from the chair, and endeavoured to get up again with the pail of water. He intended to hang it from the hook, dangling over the head of Tommy Brock, in order to make a sort of shower-bath, worked by a string, through the window.

But naturally being a thin-legged person (though vindictive and sandy whiskered)—he was quite unable to lift the heavy weight to the level of the hook and rope. He very nearly over-balanced himself.

The snores became more and more apoplectic. One of Tommy Brock's hind legs twitched under the blanket, but still he slept on peacefully.

Mr. Tod and the pail descended from the chair without accident. After considerable thought, he emptied the water into a wash-basin and jug. The empty pail was not too heavy for him; he slung it up wobbling over the head of Tommy Brock.

Surely there never was such a sleeper! Mr. Tod got up and down, down and up on the chair.

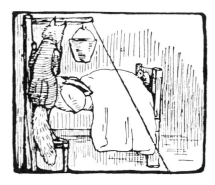

As he could not lift the whole pailful of water at once, he fetched a milk jug, and ladled quarts of water into the pail by degrees. The pail got fuller and fuller, and swung like a pendulum. Occasionally a drop splashed over; but still Tommy Brock snored regularly and never moved,—except one eye.

At last Mr. Tod's preparations were complete. The pail was full of water; the rope was tightly strained over the top of the bed, and across the window-sill to the tree outside.

"It will make a great mess in my bedroom; but I could never

sleep in that bed again without a spring cleaning of some sort," said Mr. Tod.

Mr. Tod took a last look at the badger and softly left the room. He went out of the house, shutting the front door. The rabbits heard his footsteps over the tunnel.

He ran round behind the house, intending to undo the rope in order to let fall the pailful of water upon Tommy Brock—

"I will wake him up with an unpleasant surprise," said Mr. Tod.

The moment he had gone, Tommy Brock got up in a hurry;

he rolled Mr. Tod's dressing-gown into a bundle, put it into the bed beneath the pail of water instead of himself, and left the room also— grinning immensely.

He went into the kitchen, lighted the fire and boiled the kettle; for the moment he did not trouble himself to cook the baby rabbits.

When Mr. Tod got to the tree, he found that the weight and strain had dragged the knot so tight that it was past untying. He was obliged to gnaw it with his teeth. He chewed and gnawed for more than twenty minutes. At last the rope gave way with such a sudden jerk that it nearly pulled his teeth out, and quite knocked him over backwards.

Inside the house there was a great crash and splash, and the noise of a pail rolling over and over.

But no screams. Mr. Tod was mystified; he sat quite still, and listened attentively. Then he peeped in at the window. The water was dripping from the bed, the pail had rolled into a corner.

In the middle of the bed under the blanket, was a wet flattened *something*—much dinged in, in the middle where the pail had caught it (as it were across the tummy.) Its head was covered by the wet blanket and it was *not snoring any longer.*

There was nothing stirring, and no sound except the drip, drop, drop drip of water trickling from the mattress.

Mr. Tod watched it for half an hour; his eyes glistened.

Then he cut a caper, and became so bold that he even tapped at the window; but the bundle never moved.

Yes—there was no doubt about it—it had turned out even better than he had planned; the pail had hit poor old Tommy Brock, and killed him dead!

"I will bury that nasty person in the hole which he has dug. I will bring my bedding out, and dry it in the sun," said Mr. Tod.

"I will wash the tablecloth and spread it on the grass in the sun to bleach. And the blanket must be hung up in the wind; and the bed must be thoroughly disinfected, and aired with a warming-pan; and warmed with a hot-water bottle.

"I will get soft soap, and monkey soap, and all sorts of soap; and soda and scrubbing brushes; and persian powder; and carbolic to remove the smell. I must have a disinfecting. Perhaps I may have to burn sulphur."

He hurried round the house to get a shovel from the kitchen— "First I will arrange the hole—then I will drag out that person in the blanket . . . "

He opened the door . . .

Tommy Brock was sitting at Mr. Tod's kitchen table, pouring out tea from Mr. Tod's tea-pot into Mr. Tod's tea-cup. He was quite dry himself and grinning; and he threw the cup of scalding tea all over Mr. Tod.

Then Mr. Tod rushed upon Tommy Brock, and Tommy Brock grappled with Mr. Tod amongst the broken crockery, and there was a terrific battle all over the kitchen. To the rabbits underneath it sounded as if the floor would give way at each crash of falling furniture.

They crept out of their tunnel, and hung about amongst the rocks and bushes, listening anxiously.

Inside the house the racket was fearful.

The rabbit babies in the oven woke up trembling; perhaps it was fortunate they were shut up inside.

Everything was upset except the kitchen table.

And everything was broken, except the mantelpiece and the kitchen fender. The crockery was smashed to atoms.

The chairs were broken, and the window, and the clock fell with a crash, and there were handfuls of Mr. Tod's sandy whiskers.

The vases fell off the mantelpiece, the canisters fell off the shelf; the kettle fell off the hob. Tommy Brock put his foot in a jar of raspberry jam.

And the boiling water out of the kettle fell upon the tail of Mr. Tod.

When the kettle fell, Tommy Brock, who was still grinning, happened to be uppermost; and he rolled Mr. Tod over and over like a log, out at the door.

Then the snarling and worrying went on outside; and they rolled over the bank, and down hill, bumping over the rocks.

There will never be any love lost between Tommy Brock and Mr. Tod.

As soon as the coast was clear, Peter Rabbit and Benjamin Bunny came out of the bushes—

"Now for it! Run in, Cousin Benjamin! Run in and get them! while I watch at the door."

But Benjamin was frightened—

"Oh; oh! they are coming back!"

"No they are not."

"Yes they are!"

"What dreadful bad language! I think they have fallen down the stone quarry."

Still Benjamin hesitated, and Peter kept pushing him—

"Be quick, it's all right. Shut the oven door, Cousin Benjamin, so that he won't miss them."

Decidedly there were lively doings in Mr. Tod's kitchen!

At home in the rabbit hole, things had not been quite comfortable.

After quarrelling at supper, Flopsy and old Mr. Bouncer had passed a sleepless night, and quarrelled again at breakfast. Old Mr. Bouncer could no longer deny that he had invited company into the rabbit hole; but he refused to reply to the questions and reproaches of Flopsy. The day passed heavily.

Old Mr. Bouncer, very sulky, was huddled up in a corner, barricaded with a chair. Flopsy had taken away his pipe and hidden the tobacco. She had been having a complete turn out and spring-cleaning, to relieve her feelings. She had just finished.

Old Mr. Bouncer, behind his chair, was wondering anxiously what she would do next.

In Mr. Tod's kitchen, amongst the wreckage, Benjamin Bunny picked his way to the oven nervously, through a thick cloud of dust. He opened the oven door, felt inside, and found something warm and wriggling. He lifted it out carefully, and rejoined Peter Rabbit.

"I've got them! Can we get away? Shall we hide, Cousin Peter?"

Peter pricked his ears; distant sounds of fighting still echoed in the wood.

Five minutes afterwards two breathless rabbits came scuttering away down Bull Banks, half carrying, half dragging a sack between them, bumpetty bump over the grass. They reached home safely and burst into the rabbit hole.

Great was old Mr. Bouncer's relief and Flopsy's joy when Peter and Benjamin arrived in triumph with the young family.

The rabbit-babies were rather tumbled and very hungry; they were fed and put to bed. They soon recovered.

A long new pipe and a fresh supply of rabbit tobacco was presented to Mr. Bouncer. He was rather upon his dignity; but he accepted.

Old Mr. Bouncer was forgiven, and they all had dinner. Then Peter and Benjamin told their story—but they had not waited long enough to be able to tell the end of the battle between Tommy Brock and Mr. Tod.

THE END

THE TALE OF
PIGLING BLAND

1913

ABOUT THIS BOOK

1913 was a busy year for Beatrix Potter. Despite illness, she had arrangements to make for her marriage to William Heelis and their new home, Castle Cottage, to prepare. She only just managed to finish *The Tale of Pigling Bland* for publication in that year, writing to a friend, "I'm afraid it was done in an awful hurry and scramble." Nevertheless, it is a delightful story, which had been germinating in Beatrix's mind for some years. In 1909 she had described the sale of two of the Hill Top farm pigs in a letter to Milly Warne. "Their appetites were fearful – five meals a day and not satisfied." Pig-wig, too, was a real animal, a black Berkshire pig whom Beatrix kept as a pet. She dedicated the story to the two children of the farmer who supplied her with Pig-wig, "For Cecily and Charlie. A Tale of The Christmas Pig."

ONCE upon a time there was an old pig called Aunt Pettitoes. She had eight of a family: four little girl pigs, called Cross-patch, Suck-suck, Yock-yock and Spot; and four little boy pigs, called Alexander, Pigling Bland, Chin-chin and Stumpy. Stumpy had had an accident to his tail.

The eight little pigs had very fine appetites. "Yus, yus, yus! they eat and indeed they *do* eat!" said Aunt Pettitoes, looking at her family with pride.

Suddenly there were fearful squeals; Alexander had squeezed inside the hoops of the pig trough and stuck.

Aunt Pettitoes and I dragged him out by the hind legs.

Chin-chin was already in disgrace; it was washing day, and he had eaten a piece of soap. And presently in a basket of clean clothes, we found another dirty little pig. "Tchut, tut, tut! which ever is this?" grunted Aunt Pettitoes.

283

Now all the pig family are pink, or pink with black spots, but this pig child was smutty black all over; when it had been popped into a tub, it proved to be Yock-yock.

I went into the garden; there I found Cross-patch and Suck-suck rooting up carrots. I whipped them myself and led them out by the ears. Cross-patch tried to bite me.

"Aunt Pettitoes, Aunt Pettitoes! You are a worthy person, but your family is not well brought up. Every one of them has been in mischief except Spot and Pigling Bland."

"Yus, yus!" sighed Aunt Pettitoes. "And they drink bucketfuls of milk; I shall have to get another cow! Good little Spot shall stay at home to do the house-work; but the others must go. Four little boy pigs and four little girl pigs are too many altogether.

"Yus, yus, yus," said Aunt Pettitoes, "there will be more to eat without them."

So Chin-chin and Suck-suck went away in a wheel-barrow, and Stumpy, Yock-yock and Cross-patch rode away in a cart.

And the other two little boy pigs, Pigling Bland and Alexander, went to market. We brushed their coats, we curled their tails and washed their little faces, and wished them good-bye in the yard.

Aunt Pettitoes wiped her eyes with a large pocket handkerchief, then she wiped Pigling Bland's nose and shed tears; then she passed the handkerchief to Spot. Aunt Pettitoes sighed and grunted, and addressed those little pigs as follows:

"Now Pigling Bland, son Pigling Bland, you must go to market. Take your brother Alexander by the hand. Mind your Sunday clothes, and remember to blow your nose"—(Aunt Pettitoes passed round the handkerchief again)—"beware of

traps, hen roosts, bacon and eggs; always walk upon your hind legs." Pigling Bland, who was a sedate little pig, looked solemnly at his mother, a tear trickled down his cheek.

Aunt Pettitoes turned to the other—"Now son Alexander take the hand"—"Wee, wee, wee!" giggled Alexander—"take the hand of your brother Pigling Bland, you must go to market. Mind—""Wee, wee, wee!" interrupted Alexander again. "You put me out," said Aunt Pettitoes—"Observe sign-posts and milestones; do not gobble herring bones—""And remember," said I impressively, "if you once cross the county boundary you cannot come back. Alexander, you are not attending.

Here are two licences permitting two pigs to go to market in Lancashire. Attend, Alexander. I have had no end of trouble in getting these papers from the policeman."

Pigling Bland listened gravely; Alexander was hopelessly volatile.

I pinned the papers, for safety, inside their waistcoat pockets;

Aunt Pettitoes gave to each a little bundle, and eight conversation peppermints with appropriate moral sentiments in screws of paper. Then they started.

Pigling Bland and Alexander trotted along steadily for a mile; at least Pigling Bland did. Alexander made the road half as long again by skipping from side to side. He danced about and pinched his brother, singing—

"This pig went to market, this pig stayed at home,
This pig had a bit of meat—

"Let's see what they have given *us* for dinner, Pigling?"

Pigling Bland and Alexander sat down and untied their bundles. Alexander gobbled up his dinner in no time; he had already eaten all his own peppermints. "Give me one of yours, please, Pigling." "But I wish to preserve them for emergencies," said Pigling Bland doubtfully. Alexander went into squeals of laughter. Then he pricked Pigling with the pin that had fastened his pig paper; and when Pigling slapped him he dropped the pin, and tried to take Pigling's pin, and the papers got mixed up. Pigling Bland reproved Alexander.

But presently they made it up again, and trotted away together, singing—

> "Tom, Tom, the piper's son, stole a pig
> and away he ran!
> But all the tune that he could play,
> was 'Over the hills and far away'!"

"What's that, young sirs? Stole a pig? Where are your licences?" said the policeman. They had nearly run against him round a corner. Pigling Bland pulled out his paper; Alexander, after fumbling, handed over something scrumply—

"To $2\frac{1}{2}$ oz. conversation sweeties at three farthings—What's this? This ain't a licence." Alexander's nose lengthened visibly, he had lost it. "I had one, indeed I had, Mr. Policeman!"

"It's not likely they let you start without. I am passing the farm. You may walk with me." "Can I come back too?" inquired Pigling Bland. "I see no reason, young sir; your paper is all right." Pigling Bland did not like going on alone, and it was beginning to rain.

But it is unwise to argue with the police; he gave his brother a peppermint, and watched him out of sight.

To conclude the adventures of Alexander—the policeman sauntered up to the house about tea time, followed by a damp subdued little pig. I disposed of Alexander in the neighbourhood; he did fairly well when he had settled down.

Pigling Bland went on alone dejectedly; he came to cross-roads and a sign-post—"To Market Town, 5 miles", "Over the Hills, 4 miles", "To Pettitoes Farm, 3 miles".

Pigling Bland was shocked, there was little hope of sleeping in Market Town, and to-morrow was the hiring fair; it was deplorable to think how much time had been wasted by the frivolity of Alexander.

He glanced wistfully along the road towards the hills, and then set off walking obediently the other way, buttoning up his coat against the rain. He had never wanted to go; and the idea of standing all by himself in a crowded market, to be stared at, pushed, and  hired by some big strange farmer was very disagreeable—

"I wish I could have a little garden and grow potatoes," said Pigling Bland.

He put his cold hand in his pocket and felt his paper, he put his other hand in his other pocket and felt another paper— Alexander's! Pigling squealed; then ran back frantically, hoping to overtake Alexander and the policeman.

He took a wrong turn—several wrong turns, and was quite lost.

It grew dark, the wind whistled, the trees creaked and groaned.

Pigling Bland became frightened and cried "Wee, wee, wee! I can't find my way home!"

After an hour's wandering he got out of the wood; the moon shone through the clouds, and Pigling Bland saw a country that was new to him.

The road crossed a moor; below was a wide valley with a river twinkling in the moonlight, and beyond, in misty distance, lay the hills.

He saw a small wooden hut, made his way to it, and crept inside—"I am afraid it *is* a hen house, but what can I do?" said Pigling Bland, wet and cold and quite tired out.

"Bacon and eggs, bacon and eggs!" clucked a hen on a perch.

"Trap, trap, trap! cackle, cackle, cackle!" scolded the disturbed cockerel. "To market, to market! jiggetty jig!" clucked a broody white hen roosting next to him. Pigling Bland, much alarmed, determined to leave at daybreak. In the meantime, he and the hens fell asleep.

In less than an hour they were all awakened. The owner, Mr. Peter Thomas Piperson, came with a lantern and a hamper to catch six fowls to take to market in the morning.

He grabbed the white hen roosting next to the cock; then his eye fell upon Pigling Bland, squeezed up in a corner. He made a singular remark—"Hallo, here's another!"—seized Pigling by the scruff of the neck, and dropped him into the hamper. Then he dropped in five more dirty, kicking, cackling hens upon the top of Pigling Bland.

The hamper containing six fowls and a young pig was no light weight; it was taken down hill, unsteadily, with jerks. Pigling, although nearly scratched to pieces, contrived to hide the papers and peppermints inside his clothes.

At last the hamper was bumped down upon a kitchen floor, the lid was opened, and Pigling was lifted out. He looked up, blinking, and saw an offensively ugly elderly man, grinning from ear to ear.

"This one's come of himself, whatever," said Mr. Piperson, turning Pigling's pockets inside out. He pushed the hamper into a corner, threw a sack over it to keep the hens quiet, put a pot on the fire, and unlaced his boots.

Pigling Bland drew forward a coppy stool, and sat on the edge of it, shyly warming his hands. Mr. Piperson pulled off a boot

and threw it against the wainscot at the futher end of the kitchen.

There was a smothered noise—"Shut up!" said Mr. Piperson. Pigling Bland warmed his hands, and eyed him.

Mr. Piperson pulled off the
other boot and flung it after
the first, there was again
a curious noise—"Be quiet,
will ye?" said Mr. Piperson.
Pigling Bland sat on the very
edge of the coppy stool.

Mr. Piperson fetched meal from a
chest and made porridge. It seemed to Pigling that something at
the further end of the kitchen was taking a suppressed interest in
the cooking, but he was too hungry to be troubled by noises.

Mr. Piperson poured out three platefuls: for himself, for Pigling,
and a third—after glaring at Pigling—he put away with much
scuffling, and locked up. Pigling Bland ate his supper discreetly.

After supper Mr. Piperson consulted an almanac, and felt Pigling's ribs; it was too late in the season for curing bacon, and he grudged his meal. Besides, the hens had seen this pig.

He looked at the small remains of a flitch, and then looked undecidedly at Pigling. "You may sleep on the rug," said Mr. Peter Thomas Piperson.

Pigling Bland slept like a top. In the morning Mr. Piperson made more porridge; the weather was warmer. He looked to see how much meal was left in the chest, and seemed dissatisfied— "You'll likely be moving on again?" said he to Pigling Bland.

Before Pigling could reply, a neighbour, who was giving Mr. Piperson and the hens a lift, whistled from the gate. Mr. Piperson hurried out with the hamper, enjoining Pigling to shut the door behind him and not meddle with nought; or "I'll come back and skin ye!" said Mr. Piperson.

It crossed Pigling's mind that if *he* had asked for a lift, too, he might still have been in time for market.

But he distrusted Peter Thomas.

After finishing breakfast at his leisure, Pigling had a look round the cottage; everything was locked up. He found some potato peelings in a bucket in the back kitchen. Pigling ate the peel, and washed up the porridge plates in the bucket.

He sang while he worked—

"Tom with his pipe made such a noise,
He called up all the girls and boys—
And they all ran to hear him play
'Over the hills and far away'!"

Suddenly a little smothered voice chimed in—

"Over the hills and a great way off,
The wind shall blow my top knot off!"

Pigling Bland put down a plate which he was wiping, and listened.

After a long pause, Pigling went on tip-toe and peeped round the door into the front kitchen. There was nobody there.

After another pause, Pigling approached the door of the locked cupboard, and snuffed at the key-hole. It was quite quiet.

After another long pause, Pigling pushed a peppermint under the door. It was sucked in immediately.

In the course of the day Pigling pushed in all the remaining six peppermints.

When Mr. Piperson returned, he found Pigling sitting before the fire; he had brushed up the hearth and put on the pot to boil; the meal was not get-at-able.

Mr. Piperson was very affable; he slapped Pigling on the back, made lots of porridge and forgot to lock the meal chest. He did lock the cupboard door; but without properly shutting it. He went to bed early, and told Pigling upon no account to disturb him next day before twelve o'clock.

Pigling Bland sat by the fire, eating his supper.

All at once at his elbow, a little voice spoke—"My name is Pig-wig. Make me more porridge, please!" Pigling Bland jumped, and looked round.

A perfectly lovely little black Berkshire pig stood smiling beside him. She had twinkly little screwed-up eyes, a double chin, and a short turned-up nose.

She pointed at Pigling's plate; he hastily gave it to her, and fled to the meal chest. "How did you come here?" asked Pigling Bland.

"Stolen," replied Pig-wig, with her mouth full. Pigling helped himself to meal without scruple. "What for?" "Bacon, hams," replied Pig-wig cheerfully.

"Why on earth don't you run away?" exclaimed the horrified Pigling.

"I shall after supper," said Pig-wig decidedly.

Pigling Bland made more porridge and watched her shyly.

She finished a second plate, got up, and looked about her, as though she were going to start.

"You can't go in the dark," said Pigling Bland.

Pig-wig looked anxious.

"Do you know your way by daylight?"

"I know we can see this little white house from the hills across the river. Which way are *you* going, Mr. Pig?"

"To market—I have two pig papers. I might take you to the bridge; if you have no objection," said Pigling much confused and sitting on the edge of his coppy stool. Pig-wig's gratitude was such and she asked so many questions that it became embarrassing to Pigling Bland.

He was obliged to shut his eyes and pretend to sleep. She became quiet, and there was a smell of peppermint.

"I thought you had eaten them," said Pigling, waking suddenly.

"Only the corners," replied Pig-wig, studying the sentiments with much interest by the firelight.

"I wish you wouldn't; he might smell them through the ceiling," said the alarmed Pigling.

Pig-wig put back the sticky peppermints into her pocket; "Sing something," she demanded.

"I am sorry . . . I have toothache," said Pigling much dismayed.

"Then I will sing," replied Pig-wig.

"You will not mind if I say iddy tidditty? I have forgotten some of the words."

Pigling Bland made no objection; he sat with his eyes half shut, and watched her.

She wagged her head and rocked about, clapping time and singing in a sweet little grunty voice—

"A funny old mother pig lived in a stye,
    and three little piggies had she;
(Ti idditty idditty) umph, umph, umph!
    and the little pigs said, wee, wee!"

She sang successfully through three or four verses, only at every verse her head nodded a little lower, and her little twinkly eyes closed up.

"Those three little piggies grew peaky
and lean, and lean they might very
well be;
For somehow they couldn't say umph,
umph, umph! and they wouldn't
say wee, wee, wee!
For somehow they couldn't say—"

Pig-wig's head bobbed lower and lower, until she rolled over, a little round ball, fast asleep on the hearth-rug.

Pigling Bland, on tip-toe, covered her up with an antimacassar.

He was afraid to go to sleep himself; for the rest of the night he sat listening to the chirping of the crickets and to the snores of Mr. Piperson overhead.

Early in the morning, between dark and daylight, Pigling tied up his little bundle and woke up Pig-wig. She was excited and half-frightened. "But it's dark! How can we find our way?"

"The cock has crowed; we must start before the hens come out; they might shout to Mr. Piperson."

Pig-wig sat down again, and commenced to cry.

"Come away Pig-wig; we can see when we get used to it. Come! I can hear them clucking!"

Pigling had never said shuh! to a hen in his life, being peaceable; also he remembered the hamper.

He opened the house door quietly and shut it after them. There was no garden; the neighbourhood of Mr. Piperson's was all scratched up by fowls. They slipped away hand in hand across an untidy field to the road.

The sun rose while they were crossing the moor, a dazzle of light over the tops of the hills. The sunshine crept down the slopes into the peaceful green valleys, where little white cottages nestled in gardens and orchards.

"That's Westmorland," said Pig-wig. She dropped Pigling's hand and commenced to dance, singing—

"Tom, Tom, the piper's son, stole a pig and away he ran!
But all the tune that he could play, was 'Over the hills and far away'!"

"Come, Pig-wig, we must get to the bridge before folks are stirring." "Why do you want to go to market, Pigling?" inquired Pig-wig presently. "I don't want; I want to grow potatoes." "Have a peppermint?" said Pig-wig. Pigling Bland refused quite crossly. "Does your poor toothy hurt?" inquired Pig-wig. Pigling Bland grunted.

Pig-wig ate the peppermint herself and followed the opposite side of the road. "Pig-wig! Keep under the wall, there's a man ploughing." Pig-wig crossed over, they hurried down hill towards the county boundary.

Suddenly Pigling stopped; he heard wheels.

Slowly jogging up the road below them came a tradesman's cart. The reins flapped on the horse's back, the grocer was reading a newspaper.

"Take that peppermint out of your mouth, Pig-wig, we may have to run.

Don't say one word. Leave it to me. And in sight of the bridge!" said poor Pigling, nearly crying. He began to walk frightfully lame, holding Pig-wig's arm.

The grocer, intent upon his newspaper, might have passed them, if his horse had not shied and snorted. He pulled the cart crossways, and held down his whip. "Hallo! Where are *you* going to?"— Pigling Bland stared at him vacantly.

"Are you deaf? Are you going to market?" Pigling nodded slowly.

"I thought as much. It was yesterday. Show me your licence?"

Pigling stared at the off hind shoe of the grocer's horse which had picked up a stone.

The grocer flicked his whip—"Papers? Pig licence?" Pigling

fumbled in all his pockets, and handed up the papers. The grocer read them, but still seemed dissatisfied. "This here pig is a young lady; is her name Alexander?" Pig-wig opened her mouth and shut it again; Pigling coughed asthmatically.

The grocer ran his finger down the advertisement column of his newspaper—"Lost, stolen or strayed, 10s. reward." He looked suspiciously at Pig-wig. Then he stood up in the trap, and whistled for the ploughman.

"You wait here while I drive on and speak to him," said the grocer, gathering up the reins. He knew that pigs are slippery; but surely, such a *very* lame pig could never run!

"Not yet, Pig-wig, he will look back." The grocer did so; he saw the two pigs stock-still in the middle of the road. Then he

looked over at his horse's heels; it was lame also; the stone took some time to knock out, after he got to the ploughman.

"Now, Pig-wig, Now!" said Pigling Bland.

Never did any pigs run as these pigs ran! They raced and squealed and pelted down the long white hill towards the bridge. Little fat Pig-wig's petticoats fluttered, and her feet went pitter, patter, pitter, as she bounded and jumped.

They ran, and they ran, and they ran down the hill, and across a short cut on level green turf at the bottom, between pebble beds and rushes.

They came to the river, they came to the bridge—they crossed it hand in hand—then over the hills and far away she danced with Pigling Bland!

THE END

APPLEY DAPPLY'S
NURSERY RHYMES

1917

About This Book

Ideas for *Appley Dapply's Nursery Rhymes* had been in Beatrix Potter's mind for many years before the book was eventually published. As early as 1893, she prepared pictures of the old woman who lived in a shoe, and in 1902 she discussed further drawings with her publisher after finishing *Peter Rabbit*. Other stories were chosen however, and the book was laid aside. Beatrix wrote to Norman Warne in 1905, asking if she could call and discuss the rhymes, but his tragic death shortly afterwards meant the ideas were shelved again. Finally, Beatrix revived *Appley Dapply* in response to Warne's request for a new book in 1917. She had written the rhymes herself over a number of years, and the fact that the illustrations were painted at different times explains why some have square edges while others are vignetted, and why the style occasionally varies.

APPLEY Dapply, a little
brown mouse,
Goes to the cupboard in
somebody's house.

In somebody's cupboard
There's everything nice,
Cake, cheese, jam, biscuits,
—All charming for mice!

Appley Dapply has little
sharp eyes,
And Appley Dapply is
so fond of pies!

NOW who is this knocking
at Cottontail's door?
Tap tappit! Tap tappit!
She's heard it before?

And when she peeps out
there is nobody there,
But a present of carrots
put down on the stair.

Hark! I hear it again!
Tap, tap, tappit!
Tap tappit!
Why—I really believe it's
a little black rabbit!

OLD Mr. Pricklepin
   has never a cushion
to stick his pins in,
His nose is black and his
   beard is grey,
And he lives in an ash
   stump over the way.

YOU know the old woman
   who lived in a shoe?
And had so many children
   She didn't know what to do?

I think if she lived in
   a little shoe-house—
That little old woman was
   surely a mouse!

DIGGORY DIGGORY
   DELVET!
A little old man in
   black velvet;
He digs and he delves—
You can see for your-
   selves
The mounds dug by
   Diggory Delvet.

GRAVY and potatoes
   In a good brown
      pot—
Put them in the oven,
   and serve them very
      hot!

THERE once was an
    amiable guinea-pig,
Who brushed back his hair
    like a periwig—

He wore a sweet tie,
    As blue as the sky—

And his whiskers and buttons
    Were very big.

THE END

THE TALE OF JOHNNY TOWN~MOUSE

1918

ABOUT THIS BOOK

The Tale of Johnny Town-Mouse is set in Lake District surroundings: Johnny lives in the town of Hawkshead, as one can tell from the archway in one of the pictures, while Timmy Willie has his home in a Sawrey garden. Old Diamond, Beatrix's farm horse, pulls the carrier's cart (her favourite of all the pictures), and the cook is a local woman, Mrs. Rogerson. Johnny Town-mouse himself is based on a Doctor Parsons, who would bring his long bag of clubs (drawn in the cover picture on the previous page) to play golf with Beatrix's husband, Willie Heelis.

The theme of the tale is taken from a fable by Aesop, and Beatrix dedicated the story to "Aesop in the shadows." Her sight was failing, and she despaired of the drawings. "I *cannot* see to put colour in them." However the country pictures, in particular, are as delightful as ever.

JOHNNY TOWN-MOUSE
was born in a cupboard.
Timmy Willie was born in a
garden. Timmy Willie was a
little country mouse who went
to town by mistake in a hamper.
The gardener sent vegetables to
town once a week by carrier;
he packed them in a big
hamper.

The gardener left the hamper by the garden gate, so that the carrier could pick it up when he passed. Timmy Willie crept in through a hole in the wickerwork, and after eating some peas—Timmy Willie fell fast asleep.

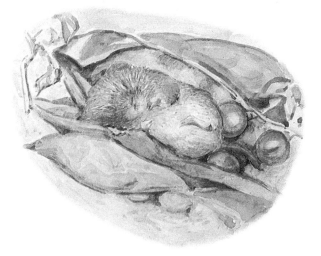

He awoke in a fright, while the hamper was being lifted into the carrier's cart. Then there was a jolting, and a clattering of horse's feet; other packages were thrown in; for miles and miles —jolt—jolt—jolt! and Timmy Willie trembled amongst the jumbled-up vegetables.

At last the cart stopped at a house, where the hamper was taken out, carried in, and set down. The cook gave the carrier sixpence; the back door banged, and the cart rumbled away. But there was no quiet; there seemed to be hundreds of carts passing. Dogs barked; boys whistled in the street; the cook laughed, the parlour maid ran up and down-stairs; and a canary sang like a steam engine.

Timmy Willie, who had lived all his life in a garden, was almost frightened to death. Presently the cook opened the hamper and began to unpack the vegetables. Out sprang the terrified Timmy Willie.

Up jumped the cook on a chair, exclaiming "A mouse! A mouse! Call the cat! Fetch me the poker, Sarah!" Timmy Willie did not wait for Sarah with the poker; he rushed along the skirting board till he came to a little hole, and in he popped.

He dropped half a foot, and crashed into the middle of a mouse dinner party, breaking three glasses.—"Who in the world is this?" inquired Johnny Town-mouse. But after the first exclamation of surprise he instantly recovered his manners.

With the utmost politeness he introduced Timmy Willie to nine other mice, all with long tails and white neck-ties. Timmy Willie's own tail was insignificant. Johnny Town-mouse and his friends noticed it; but they were too well bred to make personal remarks; only one of them asked Timmy Willie if he had ever been in a trap?

The dinner was of eight courses; not much of anything, but truly elegant. All the dishes were unknown to Timmy Willie, who would have been a little afraid of tasting them; only he was very hungry, and very anxious to behave with company manners.

The continual noise upstairs made him so nervous, that he dropped a plate. "Never mind, they don't belong to us," said Johnny.

"Why don't those youngsters come back with the dessert?" It should be explained that two young mice, who were waiting on the others, went skirmishing upstairs to the kitchen between courses. Several times they had come tumbling in, squeaking and laughing; Timmy Willie learnt with horror that they were being chased by the cat. His appetite failed, he felt faint. "Try some jelly?" said Johnny Town-mouse.

"No? Would you rather go to bed? I will show you a most comfortable sofa pillow."

The sofa pillow had a hole in it. Johnny Town-mouse quite honestly recommended it as the best bed, kept exclusively for visitors. But the sofa smelt of cat. Timmy Willie preferred to spend a miserable night under the fender.

It was just the same next day. An excellent breakfast was provided— for mice accustomed to eat bacon; but Timmy Willie had been reared on roots and salad. Johnny Town-mouse and his friends racketted about under the floors, and came boldly out all over the house in the evening. One particularly loud crash had been caused by Sarah tumbling downstairs with the tea-tray; there were crumbs and sugar and smears of jam to be collected, in spite of the cat.

Timmy Willie longed to be at home in his peaceful nest in a sunny bank. The food disagreed with him; the noise prevented him from sleeping. In a few days he grew so thin that Johnny Town-mouse noticed it, and questioned him. He listened to Timmy Willie's story and inquired about the garden. "It sounds rather a dull place? What do you do when it rains?"

"When it rains, I sit in my little sandy burrow and shell corn and seeds from my Autumn store. I peep out at the throstles and blackbirds on the lawn, and my friend Cock Robin. And when the sun comes out again, you should see my garden and the flowers—roses and pinks and pansies—no noise except the birds and bees, and the lambs in the meadows."

"There goes that cat again!" exclaimed Johnny Town-mouse. When they had taken refuge in the coal-cellar he resumed the conversation: "I confess I am a little disappointed; we have endeavoured to entertain you, Timothy William."

"Oh yes, yes, you have been most kind; but I do feel so ill," said Timmy Willie.

"It may be that your teeth and digestion are unaccustomed to our food; perhaps it might be wiser for you to return in the hamper."

"Oh? Oh!" cried Timmy Willie.

"Why of course for the matter of that we could have sent you back last week," said Johnny rather huffily—"Did you not know that the hamper goes back empty on Saturdays?"

So Timmy Willie said good-bye to his new friends, and hid in the hamper with a crumb of cake and a withered cabbage leaf; and after much jolting, he was set down safely in his own garden.

Sometimes on Saturdays he went to look at the hamper lying by the gate, but he knew better than to get in again. And nobody got out, though Johnny Town-mouse had half promised a visit.

The winter passed; the sun came out again; Timmy Willie sat by his burrow warming his little fur coat and sniffing the smell of violets and spring grass.

He had nearly forgotten his visit to town. When up the sandy path all spick and span with a brown leather bag came Johnny Town-mouse!

Timmy Willie received him with open arms. "You have come at the best of all the year, we will have herb pudding and sit in the sun."

"H'm'm! It is a little damp," said Johnny Town-mouse, who was carrying his tail under his arm, out of the mud.

"What is that fearful noise?" he started violently.

"That?" said Timmy Willie. "That is only a cow; I will beg a little milk, they are quite harmless, unless they happen to lie down upon you. How are all our friends?"

Johnny's account was rather middling. He explained why he was paying his visit so early in the season; the family had gone to the sea-side for Easter; the cook was doing spring cleaning, on board wages, with particular instructions to clear out the mice. There were four kittens, and the cat had killed the canary.

"They say we did it; but I know better," said Johnny Town-mouse. "Whatever is that fearful racket?"

"That is only the lawn-mower; I will fetch some of the grass clippings presently to make your bed. I am sure you had better settle in the country, Johnny."

"H'm'm—we shall see by Tuesday week; the hamper is stopped while they are at the sea-side."

"I am sure you will never want to live in town again," said Timmy Willie.

But he did. He went back in the very next hamper of vegetables; he said it was too quiet!!

One place suits one person, another place suits another person. For my part I prefer to live in the country, like Timmy Willie.

THE END

CECILY PARSLEY'S NURSERY RHYMES

1922

About This Book

Beatrix Potter's second collection of nursery rhymes has roots stretching just as far back as her first, *Appley Dapply*. "The Guinea-Pigs' Garden" verses were first illustrated in 1893, when Beatrix borrowed her neighbour's guinea-pigs to paint. She made a little booklet of the Cecily Parsley poem in 1897, and a manuscript of "Ninny Nanny Netticoat", which was based on an old rhyme, also exists from that year. Her publishers pressed Beatrix for another book of rhymes following the success of *Appley Dapply*, but she was reluctant. "People worry me for just one or two more books, but my eyes are getting weak, and I am tired of doing them." *Cecily Parsley's Nursery Rhymes* was eventually published in 1922, dedicated to "Little Peter in New Zealand." He was the nephew of one of her New Zealand readers, who had been orphaned at the age of two during the First World War.

CECILY PARSLEY lived in a pen,
  And brewed good ale for gentlemen;

Gentlemen came every day,
Till Cecily Parsley ran away.

333

GOOSEY, goosey, gander,
     Whither will you wander?
Upstairs and downstairs,
     And in my lady's chamber!

THIS pig went to market;
     This pig stayed at home;

This pig had a bit of meat;

And this pig had none;

This little pig cried
"Wee! wee! wee!
I can't find my way
home."

PUSSY-CAT sits by the fire;
    How should she be fair?
In walks the little dog,
    Says "Pussy! are you there?"

"How do you do, Mistress Pussy?
    Mistress Pussy, how do you do?"
"I thank you kindly, little dog,
    I fare as well as you!"

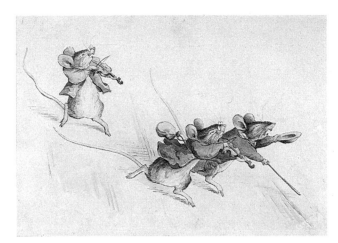

THREE blind mice, three blind mice,
   See how they run!
They all run after the farmer's wife,
And she cut off their tails with a carving knife,
Did ever you see such a thing in your life
   As three blind mice!

BOW, wow, wow!
   Whose dog art thou?
"I'm little Tom Tinker's dog,
   Bow, wow, wow!"

WE have a little garden,
    A garden of our own,
And every day we water
    there
The seeds that we have
    sown.

We love our little garden,
    And tend it with such care,
You will not find a faded leaf
    Or blighted blossom there.

NINNY NANNY
    NETTICOAT,
In a white petticoat,
    With a red nose,—
The longer she stands,
    The shorter she grows.

THE END

The Tale of
Little Pig Robinson

1930

ABOUT THIS BOOK

When Beatrix Potter was seventeen she spent a holiday at Ilfracombe in Devon with her family, where the long flight of steps leading down to the harbour gave her an idea for a story. This story was developed in 1901 and 1902, but not fully worked up until shortly before the book was published many years later in 1930. Beatrix had had a longer book, *The Fairy Caravan*, published in America, and her American publisher wanted another story. *The Tale of Little Pig Robinson* was thus published simultaneously in Britain and America, though the American edition contains more black-and-white pictures than the English. Beatrix had sketched a number of seaside towns for the book pictures while on holiday: "Stymouth" was Sidmouth in Devon, the ships were drawn in Teignmouth Harbour, the high sheds for drying nets came from Hastings in Sussex, and Lyme Regis, Dorset, was the scene of other views.

CHAPTER I

WHEN I was a child I used to go to the seaside for the holidays. We stayed in a little town where there was a harbour and fishing boats and fishermen. They sailed away to catch herrings in nets. When the boats came back home again some had only caught a few herrings. Others had caught so many that they could not all be unloaded on to the quay. Then horses and carts were driven into the shallow water at low tide to meet the heavily laden boats. The fish were shovelled over the side of the boat into the carts, and taken to the railway station, where a special train of fish trucks was waiting.

Great was the excitement when the fishing boats returned with a good catch of herrings. Half the people in the town ran down to the quay, including cats.

There was a white cat called Susan who never missed meeting the boats. She belonged to the wife of an old fisherman named Sam. The wife's name was Betsy. She had rheumatics, and she had no family except Susan and five hens. Betsy sat by the fire; her back ached; she said "Ow! Ow!" whenever she had to put coal on, and stir the pot. Susan sat opposite to Betsy. She felt sorry for Betsy; she wished she knew how to put the coal on and stir the pot. All day long they sat by the fire, while Sam was away fishing. They had a cup of tea and some milk.

"Susan," said Betsy, "I can hardly stand up. Go to the front gate and look out for Master's boat."

Susan went out and came back. Three or four times she went out into the garden. At last, late in the afternoon, she saw the sails of the fishing fleet, coming in over the sea.

"Go down to the harbour; ask Master for six herrings; I will cook them for supper. Take my basket, Susan."

Susan took the basket; also she borrowed Betsy's bonnet and little plaid shawl. I saw her hurrying down to the harbour.

Other cats were coming out of the cottages, and running down the steep streets that lead to the sea front. Also ducks. I remember that they were most peculiar ducks with top-knots that looked like Tam-o'-Shanter caps. Everybody was hurrying to meet the boats—nearly everybody. I only met one person, a dog called Stumpy, who was going the opposite way. He was carrying a paper parcel in his mouth.

Some dogs do not care for fish. Stumpy had been to the butcher's to buy mutton chops for himself and Bob and Percy and Miss Rose. Stumpy was a large, serious, well-behaved brown dog with a short tail. He lived with Bob the retriever and Percy the cat and Miss Rose who kept house. Stumpy had belonged to a very rich old gentleman; and when the old gentleman died he left money to Stumpy—ten shillings a week for the rest of Stumpy's life. So that was why Stumpy and Bob and Percy the cat all lived together in a pretty little house.

Susan with her basket met Stumpy at the corner of Broad Street. Susan made a curtsy. She would have stopped to inquire after Percy, only she was in a hurry to meet the boat. Percy was lame; he had hurt his foot. It had been trapped under the wheel of a milk cart.

Stumpy looked at Susan out of the corner of his eye; he

wagged his tail, but he did not stop. He could not bow or say "good afternoon" for fear of dropping the parcel of mutton chops. He turned out of Broad Street into Woodbine Lane, where he lived; he pushed open the front door and disappeared into a house. Presently there was a smell of cooking, and I have no doubt that Stumpy and Bob and Miss Rose enjoyed their mutton chops.

Percy could not be found at dinner time. He had slipped out of the window, and, like all the other cats in the town, he had gone to meet the fishing boats.

Susan hurried along Broad Street and took the short cut to the harbour, down a steep flight of steps. The ducks had wisely gone another way, round by the sea front. The steps were too steep and slippery for anyone less sure-footed than a cat. Susan went down quickly and easily. There were forty-three steps, rather dark and slimy, between high backs of houses.

A smell of ropes and pitch and a good deal of noise came up from below. At the bottom of the steps was the quay, or landing-place, beside the inner harbour.

The tide was out; there was no water; the vessels rested on the dirty mud. Several ships were moored beside the quay; others were anchored inside the breakwater.

Near the steps, coal was being unloaded from two grimy colliers called the "Margery Dawe" of Sunderland, and the "Jenny Jones" of Cardiff. Men ran along planks with wheel-barrowfuls of coal; coal scoops were swung ashore by cranes, and emptied with loud thumping and rattling.

Farther along the quay, another ship called the "Pound of Candles" was taking a mixed cargo on board. Bales, casks, packing-cases, barrels—all manner of goods were being stowed into the hold; sailors and stevedores shouted; chains rattled and clanked. Susan waited for an opportunity to slip past the noisy crowd. She watched a cask of cider that bobbed and swung in the air, on its passage from the quay to the deck of the "Pound of Candles". A yellow cat who sat in the rigging was also watching the cask.

The rope ran through the pulley; the cask went down

bobbitty on to the deck, where a sailor man was waiting for it. Said the sailor down below:

"Look out! Mind your head, young sir! Stand out of the way!"

"Wee, wee, wee!" grunted a small pink pig, scampering round the deck of the "Pound of Candles".

The yellow cat in the rigging watched the small pink pig. The yellow cat in the rigging looked across at Susan on the quay. The yellow cat winked.

Susan was surprised to see a pig on board a ship. But she was in a hurry. She threaded her way along the quay, amongst coal and cranes, and men wheeling hand-trucks, and noises, and smells. She passed the fish auction, and fish boxes, and fish sorters, and barrels that women were filling with herrings and salt.

Seagulls swooped and screamed. Hundreds of fish boxes and tons of fresh fish were being loaded into the hold of a small steamer. Susan was glad to get away from the crowd, down a much shorter flight of steps on to the shore of the outer harbour. The ducks arrived soon afterwards, waddling and quacking. And old Sam's boat, the "Betsy Timmins", last of the herring fleet and heavy laden, came in round the breakwater; and drove her blunt nose into the shingle.

Sam was in high spirits; he had had a big catch. He and his mate and two lads commenced to unload their fish into carts, as the tide was too low to float the fishing boat up to the quay. The boat was full of herrings.

But, good luck or bad luck, Sam never failed to throw a handful of herrings to Susan.

"Here's for the two old girls and a hot supper! Catch them, Susan! Honest now! Here's a broken fish for you! Now take the others to Betsy."

The ducks were dabbling and gobbling; the seagulls were screaming and swooping. Susan climbed the steps with her basket of herrings and went home by back streets.

Old Betsy cooked two herrings for herself and Susan, another two for Sam's supper when he came in. Then she went to bed with a hot bottle wrapped in a flannel petticoat to help her rheumatics.

Sam ate his supper and smoked a pipe by the fire; and then he went to bed. But Susan sat a long time by the fire, considering. She considered many things—fish, and ducks, and Percy with a lame foot, and dogs that eat mutton chops, and the yellow cat on the ship, and the pig. Susan thought it strange to see a pig upon a ship called the "Pound of Candles". The mice peeped out under the cupboard door. The cinders fell together on the hearth. Susan purred gently in her sleep and dreamed of fish and pigs. She could not understand that pig on board a ship. But I know all about him!

CHAPTER II

YOU remember the song about the Owl and the Pussy Cat and their beautiful pea-green boat? How they took some honey and plenty of money, wrapped up in a five pound note?

"They sailed away, for a year and a day,
To the land where the Bong tree grows—
And, there in a wood, a piggy-wig stood,
With a ring at the end of his nose—his nose,
With a ring at the end of his nose."

Now I am going to tell you the story of that pig, and why he went to live in the land of the Bong tree.

When that pig was little he lived in Devonshire, with his aunts, Miss Dorcas and Miss Porcas, at a farm called Piggery Porcombe. Their cosy thatched cottage was in an orchard at the top of a steep red Devonshire lane.

The soil was red, the grass was green; and far away below in the distance they could see red cliffs and a bit of bright blue sea. Ships with white sails sailed over the sea into the harbour of Stymouth.

I have often remarked that the Devonshire farms have very strange names. If you had ever seen Piggery Porcombe you would think that the people who lived there were very queer too! Aunt Dorcas was a stout speckled pig who kept hens. Aunt Porcas was a large smiling black pig who took in washing. We shall not hear very much about them in this story. They led prosperous uneventful lives, and their end was bacon. But their nephew Robinson had the most peculiar adventures that ever happened to a pig.

Little pig Robinson was a charming little fellow; pinky white with small blue eyes, fat cheeks and a double chin,

and a turned-up nose, with a real silver ring in it. Robinson could see that ring if he shut one eye and squinted sideways.

He was always contented and happy. All day long he ran about the farm, singing little songs to himself, and grunting "Wee, wee, wee!" His aunts missed those little songs sadly after Robinson had left them.

"Wee? Wee? Wee?" he answered when anybody spoke to him. "Wee? Wee? Wee?" listening with his head on one side and one eye screwed up.

Robinson's old aunts fed him and petted him and kept him on the trot.

"Robinson! Robinson!" called Aunt Dorcas. "Come quick! I hear a hen clucking. Fetch me the egg; don't break it now!"

"Wee, wee, wee!" answered Robinson, like a little Frenchman.

"Robinson! Robinson! I've dropped a clothes peg, come and pick it up for me!" called Aunt Porcas from the drying green (she being almost too fat to stoop down and pick up anything).

"Wee, wee, wee!" answered Robinson.

Both the aunts were very, very stout. And the stiles in the neighbourhood of Stymouth are narrow. The footpath from Piggery Porcombe crosses many fields; a red trodden track between short green grass and daisies. And wherever the footpath crosses over from one field to another field, there is sure to be a stile in the hedge.

"It is not me that is too stout; it is the stiles that are too thin," said Aunt Dorcas to Aunt Porcas. "Could you manage to squeeze through them if I stayed at home?"

"I could *not*. Not for two years I could *not,*" replied Aunt Porcas. "Aggravating, it *is* aggravating of that carrier man, to go and upset his donkey cart the day before market day. And eggs at two and tuppence a dozen! How far do you call it to walk all the way round by the road instead of crossing the fields?"

"Four miles if it's one," sighed Aunt Porcas, "and me using my last bit of soap. However shall we get our shopping done? The donkey says the cart will take a week to mend."

"Don't you think you could squeeze through the stiles if you went before dinner?"

"No, I don't, I would stick fast; and so would you," said Aunt Porcas.

"Don't you think we might venture—" commenced Aunt Dorcas.

"Venture to send Robinson by the footpath to Stymouth?" finished Aunt Porcas.

"Wee, wee, wee!" answered Robinson.

"I scarcely like to send him alone, though he is sensible for his size."

"Wee, wee, wee!" answered Robinson.

"But there is nothing else to be done," said Aunt Dorcas.

So Robinson was popped into the wash-tub with the last bit of soap. He was scrubbed and dried and polished as bright as a new pin. Then he was dressed in a little blue cotton frock and knickers, and instructed to go shopping to Stymouth with a big market basket.

In the basket were two dozen eggs, a bunch of daffodils, two spring cauliflowers; also Robinson's dinner of bread-and-jam sandwiches. The eggs and flowers and vegetables he must sell in the market, and bring back various other purchases from shopping.

"Now take care of yourself in Stymouth, Nephew Robinson. Beware of gunpowder, and ships' cooks, and pantechnicons, and sausages, and shoes, and ships, and sealing-wax. Remember the blue bag, the soap, the darning-wool—what was the other thing?" said Aunt Dorcas.

"The darning-wool, the soap, the blue bag, the yeast—what was the other thing?" said Aunt Porcas.

"Wee, wee, wee!" answered Robinson.

"The blue bag, the soap, the yeast, the darning-wool, the cabbage seed—that's five, and there ought to be six. It was two more than four because it was two too many to tie knots in the corners of his hankie, to remember by. Six to buy, it should be—"

"I have it!" said Aunt Porcas. "It was tea—tea, blue bag, soap, darning-wool, yeast, cabbage seed. You will buy most of them at Mr. Mumby's. Explain about the carrier, Robinson; tell him we will bring the washing and some more vegetables next week."

"Wee, wee, wee!" answered Robinson, setting off with the big basket.

Aunt Dorcas and Aunt Porcas stood in the porch. They watched him safely out of sight, down the field, and through the first of the many stiles. When they went back to their household tasks they were grunty and snappy with each other, because they were uneasy about Robinson.

"I wish we had not let him go. You and your tiresome blue bag!" said Aunt Dorcas.

"Blue bag, indeed! It was your darning-wool and eggs!" grumbled Aunt Porcas. "Bother that carrier man and his donkey cart! Why could not he keep out of the ditch until after market day?"

CHAPTER III

THE walk to Stymouth was a long one, in spite of going by the fields. But the footpath ran downhill all the way, and Robinson was merry. He sang his little song, for joy of the fine morning, and he chuckled "Wee, wee, wee!" Larks were singing, too, high overhead.

And higher still—high up against blue sky, the great white gulls sailed in wide circles. Their hoarse cries came softened back to earth from a great way up above. Important rooks and lively jackdaws strutted about the meadows amongst the daisies and buttercups. Lambs skipped and baa'ed; the sheep looked round at Robinson.

"Mind yourself in Stymouth, little pig," said a motherly ewe.

Robinson trotted on until he was out of breath and very hot. He had crossed five big fields, and ever so many stiles; stiles with steps; ladder stiles; stiles of wooden posts; some of them were very awkward with a heavy basket. The farm of Piggery

Porcombe was no longer in
sight when he looked back.
In the distance before him,
beyond the farmlands and
cliffs—never any nearer—
the dark blue sea rose like
a wall.

Robinson sat down to rest
beside a hedge in a sheltered
sunny spot. Yellow pussy
willow catkins were in flower
above his head; there were
primroses in hundreds on the
bank, and a warm smell of moss
and grass and steaming moist red
earth.

"If I eat my dinner now, I shall not have to carry it. Wee,
wee, wee!" said Robinson.

The walk had made him so hungry he would have liked to
eat an egg as well as the jam sandwiches; but he had been too
well brought up.

"It would spoil the two dozen," said Robinson.

He picked a bunch of primroses and tied them up with a bit
of darning-wool that Aunt Dorcas had given him for a pattern.

"I will sell them in the market for my very own self, and buy
sweeties with my pennies. How many pennies have I got?" said
Robinson, feeling in his pocket. "One from Aunt Dorcas, and
one from Aunt Porcas, and one for my primroses for my very
own self—oh, wee, wee, wee! There is somebody trotting along
the road! I shall be late for market!"

Robinson jumped up and pushed his basket through a very

narrow stile, where the footpath crossed into the public road. He saw a man on horseback. Old Mr. Pepperil came up, riding a chestnut horse with white legs. His two tall greyhounds ran before him; they looked through the bars of the gates into every field that they passed. They came bounding up to Robinson, very large and friendly; they licked his face and asked what he had got in that basket. Mr. Pepperil called them. "Here, Pirate! Here, Postboy! Come here, sir!" He did not wish to be answerable for the eggs.

The road had been recently covered with sharp new flints. Mr. Pepperil walked the chestnut horse on the grass edge, and talked to Robinson. He was a jolly old gentleman, very affable, with a red face and white whiskers. All the green fields and red ploughland between Stymouth and Piggery Porcombe belonged to him.

"Hullo, hullo! And where are you off to, little Pig Robinson?"

"Please, Mr. Pepperil, sir, I'm going to market. Wee, wee, wee!" said Robinson.

"What, all by yourself? Where are Miss Dorcas and Miss Porcas? Not ill, I trust?"

Robinson explained about the narrow stiles.

"Dear, dear! Too fat, too fat? So you are going all alone? Why don't your aunts keep a dog to run errands?"

Robinson answered all Mr. Pepperil's questions very sensibly and prettily. He showed much intelligence, and quite a good knowledge of vegetables, for one so young. He trotted along almost under the horse, looking up at its shiny chestnut coat, and the broad white girth, and Mr. Pepperil's gaiters and brown leather boots. Mr. Pepperil was pleased with Robinson; he gave him another penny. At the end of the flints, he gathered up the reins and touched the horse with his heel.

"Well, good day, little pig. Kind regards to the aunts. Mind yourself in Stymouth." He whistled for his dogs, and trotted away.

Robinson continued to walk along the road. He passed by an orchard where seven thin dirty pigs were grubbing. They had no silver rings in their noses! He crossed Styford bridge without stopping to look over the parapet at the little fishes, swimming head up stream, balanced in the sluggish current; or the white ducks that dabbled amongst floating masses of water-crowsfoot.  At Styford Mill he called to leave a message from Aunt Dorcas to the Miller about meal; the Miller's wife gave him an apple.

At the house beyond the mill, there is a big dog that barks; but the big dog Gypsy only smiled and wagged his tail at Robinson. Several carts and gigs overtook him. First, two old farmers who screwed themselves round to stare at Robinson.

They had two geese, a sack of
potatoes, and some cabbages,
sitting on the back seat of their
gig. Then an old woman passed
in a donkey cart with seven
hens, and long pink bundles
of rhubarb that had been
grown in straw under apple
barrels. Then with a rattle
and a jingle of cans came
Robinson's cousin, little
Tom Pigg, driving a strawberry roan pony, in a milk float.

He might have offered Robinson a lift, only he happened to be
going in the opposite direction;
in fact, the strawberry roan
pony was running away home.

"This little pig went to
market!" shouted little Tom
Pigg gaily, as he rattled out of
sight in a cloud of dust, leaving
Robinson standing in the road.

Robinson walked on along
the road, and presently he
came to another stile in the
opposite hedge, where the footpath followed the fields again.
Robinson got his basket through
the stile. For the first time he
felt some apprehension. In this
field there were cows; big sleek

Devon cattle, dark red like their native soil. The leader of the herd was a vicious old cow, with brass balls screwed on to the tips of her horns. She stared disagreeably at Robinson. He sidled across the meadow and got out through the farther stile as quickly as he could. Here the new trodden footpath followed round the edge of a crop of young green wheat. Someone let off a gun with a bang that made Robinson jump and cracked one of Aunt Dorcas's eggs in the basket.

A cloud of rooks and jackdaws rose cawing and scolding from the wheat. Other sounds mingled with their cries; noises of the town of Stymouth that began to come in sight through the elm trees that bordered the fields; distant noises from the station; whistling of an engine; the bump of trucks shunting; noise of workshops; the hum of a distant town; the hooter of a steamer entering the harbour. High overhead came the hoarse cry of the gulls, and the squabbling cawing of rooks, old and young, in their rookery up in the elm trees.

Robinson left the fields for the last time and joined a stream of country people on foot and in carts, all going to Stymouth Market.

CHAPTER IV

STYMOUTH is a pretty little town, situated at the mouth of the river Pigsty, whose sluggish waters slide gently into a bay sheltered by high red headlands. The town itself seems to be sliding downhill in a basin of hills, all slipping seaward into Stymouth harbour, which is surrounded by quays and the outer breakwater.

The outskirts of the town are untidy, as is frequently the case

with seaports. A straggling suburb on the western approach is
inhabited principally by goats, and persons who deal in old
iron, rags, tarred rope, and fishing nets. There are rope walks,
and washing that flaps on waggling lines above banks of stony
shingle, littered with seaweed, whelk shells and dead crabs—very
different from Aunt Porcas's clothes-line over the clean green
grass.

And there are marine stores that
sell spyglasses, and sou'westers,
and onions; and there are smells;
and curious high sheds, shaped
like sentry boxes, where they
hang up herring nets to dry;
and loud talking inside dirty
houses. It seemed a likely
place to meet a pantechnicon.
Robinson kept in the middle
of the road. Somebody in a
public-house shouted at him
through the window, "Come in,
fat pig!" Robinson took to his
heels.

The town of Stymouth itself is clean, pleasant, picturesque,
and well behaved (always excepting the harbour); but it is
extremely steep downhill. If Robinson had started one of Aunt
Dorcas's eggs rolling at the top of High Steet, it would have
rolled all the way down to the bottom; only it would have got
broken certainly against a doorstep, or underfoot. There were
crowds in the streets, as it was market day.

Indeed, it was difficult to walk about without being pushed
off the pavement; every old woman that Robinson met seemed

to have a basket as big as his own. In the roadway were fish
barrows, apple barrows, stalls with crockery and hardware,
cocks and hens riding in pony carts, donkeys with panniers, and
farmers with wagon-loads of hay. Also there was a constant
string of coal carts coming up from the docks. To a country-
bred pig, the noise was confusing and fearful.

Robinson kept his head very creditably until he got into Fore
Street, where a drover's dog was trying to turn three bullocks
into a yard, assisted by Stumpy and half the other dogs of the
town. Robinson and two other little pigs with baskets of
asparagus bolted down an alley and hid in a doorway until the
noise of bellowing and barking had passed.

When Robinson took courage to come out again into Fore
Street, he decided to follow close behind the tail of a donkey
who was carrying panniers piled
high with spring broccoli. There
was no difficulty in guessing which
road led to market. But after all
these delays it was not surprising
that the church clock struck
eleven.

Although it had been open
since ten, there were still plenty
of customers buying, and wanting
to buy, in the market hall. It
was a large, airy, light, cheerful,
covered-in place, with glass in
the roof. It was crowded, but safe
and pleasant, compared with the
jostling and racket outside in the cobble-
paved streets; at all events there was no risk of being run over.

There was a loud hum of voices; market folk cried their wares; customers elbowed and pushed round the stalls. Dairy produce, vegetables, fish, and shell fish were displayed upon the flat boards on trestles.

Robinson had found a standing place at one end of a stall where Nanny Nettigoat was selling periwinkles.

"Winkle, winkle! Wink, wink, wink! Maa, maa-a!" bleated Nanny.

Winkles were the only thing that she offered for sale, so she felt no jealousy of Robinson's eggs and primroses. She knew nothing about his cauliflowers; he had the sense to keep them in the basket under the table. He stood on an empty box quite proud and bold behind the trestle table, singing:

"Eggs, new laid! Fresh new-laid eggs! Who'll come and buy my eggs and daffodillies?"

"I will, sure," said a large brown dog with a stumpy tail, "I'll buy a dozen. My Miss Rose has sent me to market on purpose to buy eggs and butter."

"I am so sorry, I have no butter, Mr. Stumpy; but I have beautiful cauliflowers," said Robinson, lifting up the basket, after a cautious glance round at Nanny Nettigoat, who might have tried to nibble them. She was busy measuring periwinkles in a pewter mug for a duck customer in a Tam-o'-Shanter cap. "They are lovely brown eggs, except one that got cracked; I think that white pussy cat at the opposite stall is selling butter—they are beautiful cauliflowers."

"I'll buy a cauliflower, lovey, bless his little turned-up nose; did he grow them in his own garden?" said old Betsy, bustling up; her rheumatism was better; she had left Susan to keep house. "No, lovey, I don't want any eggs; I keep hens myself. A cauli-flower and a bunch of daffodils for a bow-pot, please," said Betsy.

"Wee, wee, wee!" replied Robinson.

"Here, Mrs. Perkins, come here! Look at this little pig stuck up at a stall all by himself!"

"Well, I don't know!" exclaimed Mrs. Perkins, pushing through the crowd, followed by two little girls. "Well, I never! Are they quite new-laid, sonny? Won't go off pop and spoil my Sunday dress like the eggs Mrs. Wyandotte took first prize with at five flower shows, till they popped and spoiled the judge's black silk dress? Not duck eggs, stained with coffee? That's another trick of flower shows! New-laid, guaranteed? Only you say one is cracked? Now I call that real honest: it's no worse for frying. I'll have the dozen eggs and a cauliflower, please. Look, Sarah Polly! Look at his silver nose-ring."

Sarah Polly and her little girl friend went into fits of giggling, so that Robinson blushed. He was so confused that he did not notice a lady who wanted to buy his last cauliflower, till she touched him. There was nothing else left to sell, but a bunch of primroses. After more giggling and some whispering the two little girls came back, and bought  the primroses. They gave him a peppermint, as well as the penny, which Robinson accepted; but without enthusiasm and with a preoccupied manner.

The trouble was that no sooner had he parted with the bunch of primroses than he realised that he had also sold Aunt Porcas's pattern of darning-wool. He wondered if he ought to ask for it back; but Mrs. Perkins and Sarah Polly and her little girl friend had disappeared.

Robinson, having sold everything, came out of the market hall, sucking the peppermint. There were still numbers of people coming in. As Robinson came out upon the steps his basket got caught in the shawl of an elderly sheep, who was pushing her way up. While Robinson was disentangling it, Stumpy came out. He had finished his marketing. His basket was full of heavy purchases. A responsible, trustworthy, obliging dog was Stumpy, glad to do a kindness to anybody.

When Robinson asked him the way to Mr. Mumby's, Stumpy said: "I am going home by Broad Street. Come with me, and I will show you."

"Wee, wee, wee! Oh, thank you, Stumpy!" said Robinson.

CHAPTER V

OLD Mr. Mumby was a deaf old man in spectacles, who kept a general store. He sold almost anything you can imagine, except ham—a circumstance much approved by Aunt Dorcas. It was the only general store in Stymouth where you would not find displayed upon the counter a large dish, containing strings of thin, pale-coloured, repulsively uncooked sausages, and rolled bacon hanging from the ceiling.

"What pleasure," said Aunt Dorcas feelingly—"what possible pleasure can there be in entering a shop where you knock your head against a ham? A ham that may have belonged to a dear second cousin?"

Therefore the aunts bought their sugar and tea, their blue

bag, their soap, their frying pans, matches, and mugs from old Mr. Mumby.

All these things he sold, and many more besides, and what he did not keep in stock he would obtain to order. But yeast requires to be quite fresh, he did not sell it; he advised Robinson to ask for yeast at a baker's shop. Also he said it was too late in the season to buy cabbage seed; everybody had finished sowing vegetable seeds this year. Worsted for darning he did sell; but Robinson had forgotten the colour.

Robinson bought six sticks of delightfully sticky barley sugar with his pennies, and listened carefully to Mr. Mumby's messages for Aunt Dorcas and Aunt Porcas—how they were to send some cabbages next week when the donkey cart would be mended; and how the kettle was not repaired yet, and there was a new patent box-iron he would like to recommend to Aunt Porcas.

Robinson said "Wee, wee, wee?" and listened, and little dog Tipkins who stood on a stool behind the counter, tying up grocery parcels in blue paper bags—little dog Tipkins whispered to Robinson—"Were there any rats this spring in the barn at Piggery Porcombe? And what would Robinson be doing on Saturday afternoon?"

"Wee, wee, wee!" answered Robinson.

Robinson came out of Mr. Mumby's, heavily laden. The barley sugar was comforting; but he was troubled about the darning-wool, the yeast, and the cabbage seed. He was looking about rather anxiously, when again he met old Betsy, who exclaimed:

"Bless the little piggy! Not gone home yet? Now it must not stop in Stymouth till it gets its pocket picked!"

Robinson explained his difficulty about the darning-wool.

Kind old Betsy was ready with help.

"Why, I noticed the wool round the little primrose posy; it was blue-grey colour like the last pair of socks that I knitted for Sam. Come with me to the wool shop—Fleecy Flock's wool shop. I remember the colour; well I do!" said Betsy.

Mrs. Flock was the sheep that had run against Robinson; she had bought herself three turnips and come straight home from market, for fear of missing customers while her shop was locked up.

Such a shop! Such a jumble! Wool all sorts of colours, thick wool, thin wool, fingering wool, and rug wool, bundles and bundles all jumbled up; and she could not put her hoof on anything. She was so confused and slow at finding things that Betsy got impatient.

"No, I don't want wool for slippers; *darning-wool,* Fleecy; darning-wool, same colour as I bought for my Sam's socks. Bless me, *no,* not knitting needles! Darning-wool."

"Baa, baa! Did you say white or black, m'm? Three ply, was it?"

"Oh, dear me, *grey* darning-wool on cards; not heather mixture."

"I know I have it somewhere," said Fleecy Flock helplessly, jumbling up the skeins and bundles. "Sim Ram came in this

morning with part of the Ewehampton clip; my shop is
completely cluttered up—"

It took half an hour to find the wool. If Betsy had not been
with him, Robinson never would have got it.

"It's that late, I must go home," said Betsy. "My Sam is on
shore to-day for dinner. If you take my advice you will leave
that big heavy basket with the Miss Goldfinches, and hurry
with your shopping. It's a long uphill walk home to Piggery
Porcombe."

Robinson, anxious to follow old Betsy's advice, walked
towards the Miss Goldfinches. On the way he came to a
baker's, and he remembered the yeast.

It was not the right sort of baker's, unfortunately. There was a nice bakery smell, and pastry in the window; but it was an eating house or cook shop.

When he pushed the swing door open, a man in an apron and a square white cap turned round and said, "Hullo! Is this a pork pie walking on its hind legs?"—and four rude men at a dining table burst out laughing.

Robinson left the shop in a hurry. He felt afraid to go into any other baker's shop. He was looking wistfully into another window in Fore Street when Stumpy saw him again. He had taken his own basket home, and come out on another errand. He carried Robinson's basket in his mouth and took him to a very safe baker's, where he was accustomed to buy dog biscuits for himself. There Robinson purchased Aunt Dorcas's yeast at last.

They searched in vain for cabbage seed; they were told that the only likely place was a little store on the quay, kept by a pair of wagtails.

"It is a pity I cannot go with you," said Stumpy. "My Miss Rose has sprained her ankle; she sent me to fetch twelve postage stamps, and I must take them home to her, before the post goes out. Do not try to carry this heavy basket down and up the steps; leave it with the Miss Goldfinches."

Robinson was very grateful to Stumpy. The two Miss Goldfinches kept a tea and coffee tavern which was patronized by Aunt Dorcas and the quieter market people. Over the door was a sign-board upon which was painted a fat little green bird called "The Contented Siskin", which was the name of their coffee tavern. They had a stable where the carrier's donkey rested when it came into Stymouth with the washing on Saturdays.

Robinson looked so tired that the elder Miss Goldfinch gave

him a cup of tea; but they both told him to drink it up quickly.

"Wee, wee, wee! Yock yock!" said Robinson, scalding his nose.

In spite of their respect for Aunt Dorcas, the Miss Goldfinches disapproved of his solitary shopping; and they said that the basket was far too heavy for him.

"Neither of us could lift it," said the elder Miss Goldfinch, holding out a tiny claw. "Get your cabbage seed and hurry back. Sim Ram's pony gig is still waiting in our stable. If you come back before he starts I feel sure he will give you a lift; at all events he will make room for your basket under the seat— and he passes Piggery Porcombe. Run away now!"

"Wee, wee, wee!" said Robinson.

"Whatever were they thinking of to let him come alone? He will never get home before dark," said the elder Miss Goldfinch. "Fly to the stable, Clara; tell Sim Ram's pony not to start without the basket."

The younger Miss Goldfinch flew across the yard. They were industrious, sprightly little lady birds, who kept lump sugar and thistle seed as well as tea in their tea-caddies. Their tables and china were spotlessly clean.

CHAPTER VI

STYMOUTH was full of inns; too full. The farmers usually put up their horses at the "Black Bull" or the "Horse and Farrier"; the smaller market people patronized the "Pig and Whistle".

There was another inn called the "Crown and Anchor" at the corner of Fore Street. It was much frequented by seamen;

several were lounging about the door with their hands in their pockets. One sailor-man in a blue jersey sauntered across the road, staring very hard at Robinson.

Said he—"I say little pig! do you like snuff?"

Now if Robinson had a fault, it was that he could not say "No"; not even to a hedgehog stealing eggs. As a matter of fact, snuff or tobacco made him sick. But instead of saying, "No, thank you, Mr. Man," and going straight away about his business, he shuffled his feet, half closed one eye, hung his head on one side, and grunted.

The sailor pulled out a horn snuff box and presented a small pinch to Robinson, who wrapped it up in a little bit of paper, intending to give it to Aunt Dorcas. Then, not to be outdone in politeness, he offered the sailor-man some barley sugar.

If Robinson was not fond of snuff, at all events his new acquaintance had no objection to candy.  He ate an alarming quantity. Then he pulled Robinson's ear and complimented him, and said he had five chins. He promised to take Robinson to the cabbage seed shop; and, finally, he begged to have the honour of showing him over a ship engaged in the ginger trade, commanded by Captain Barnabas Butcher, and named the "Pound of Candles".

Robinson did not very much like the name. It reminded him of tallow, of lard, of crackle and trimmings of bacon. But he allowed himself to be led away, smiling shyly, and walking on his toes. If Robinson had only known . . . that man was a ship's cook!

As they turned down the steep narrow lane, out of High Street, leading to the harbour, old Mr. Mumby at his shop door called out anxiously, "Robinson! Robinson!" But there was too much noise of carts. And a customer coming into the shop at that moment distracted his attention, and he forgot the suspicious behaviour of the sailor. Otherwise, out of regard for the family, he would undoubtedly have ordered his dog, Tipkins, to go and fetch Robinson back. As it was, he was the first person to give useful information to the police, when Robinson had been missed. But it was then too late.

Robinson and his new friend went down the long flight of steps to the harbour basin—very high steps, steep and slippery. The little pig was obliged to jump from step to step until the sailor kindly took hold of him. They walked along the quay hand in hand; their appearance seemed to cause unbounded amusement.

Robinson looked about him with much interest. He had peeped over those steps before when he had come into Stymouth in the donkey cart, but he had never ventured to go down, because the sailors are rather rough, and because they frequently have little snarling terriers on guard about their vessels.

There were ever so many ships in the harbour; the noise and bustle was almost as loud as it had been up above in the market square. A big three-masted ship called the "Goldielocks" was discharging a cargo of oranges; and farther along the quay, a small coasting brig called "Little Bo Peep" of Bristol was loading up with bales of wool belonging to the sheep of Ewehampton and Lambworthy.

Old Sim Ram, with a sheepbell and big curly horns, stood by the gangway keeping count of the bales. Every time the crane swung round and let down another bale of wool into the hold, with a scuffle of rope through the pulley, Simon Ram nodded his old head, and the bell went "tinkle tinkle, tong", and he gave a gruff bleat.

He was a person who knew Robinson by sight and ought to have warned him. He had often passed Piggery Porcombe when he drove down the lane in his gig. But his blind eye was turned towards the quay; and he had been flustered and confused by an argument with the pursers as to whether thirty-five bales of wool had been hoisted on board already or only thirty-four.

So he kept his one useful eye carefully on the wool, and counted it by the notches on his tally stick—another bale—another notch—thirty-five, thirty-six, thirty-seven; he hoped the number would come right at the finish.

His bob-tailed sheep dog, Timothy Gyp, was also acquainted with Robinson, but he was busy superintending a dog fight between an Airedale terrier belonging to the collier "Margery Dawe" and a Spanish dog belonging to the "Goldie-locks". No one took any notice of their growling and snarling, which ended in both rolling over the side of the quay and falling into the water. Robinson kept close to the sailor and held his hand very tight.

The "Pound of Candles" proved to be a good-sized schooner, newly painted and decorated with certain flags, whose significance was not understood by Robinson. She lay near the outer end of the jetty. The tide was running up fast, lapping against the ship's sides and straining the thick hawsers by which she was moored to the quay.

The crew were stowing goods on board and doing things with ropes under the direction of Captain Barnabas Butcher; a lean, brown, nautical person with a rasping voice. He banged things about and grumbled; parts of his remarks were audible on the quay. He was speaking about the tug "Sea-horse"—and about the spring tide, with a north-east wind behind it—and the baker's man and fresh vegetables—"to be shipped at eleven sharp; likewise a joint of . . ." He stopped short suddenly, and his eye lighted upon the cook and Robinson.

Robinson and the cook went on board across a shaky plank. When Robinson stepped on to the deck, he found himself face to face with a large yellow cat who was blacking boots.

The cat gave a start of surprise and dropped its blacking brush. It then began to wink and make extraordinary faces at Robinson. He had never seen a cat behave in that way before. He inquired whether it was ill. Whereupon the cook threw a boot at it, and it rushed up into the rigging. But Robinson he invited most affably to descend into the cabin, to partake of muffins and crumpets.

I do not know how many muffins Robinson consumed. He went on eating them until he fell asleep; and he went on sleeping until his stool gave a lurch, and he fell off and rolled under the table. One side of the cabin floor swung up to the ceiling; and the other side of the ceiling swung down to the floor. Plates danced about; and there were shoutings and thumpings and rattling of chains and other bad sounds.

Robinson picked himself up, feeling bumped. He scrambled up a sort of ladder-staircase on to the deck. Then he gave squeal upon squeal of horror! All round the ship there were great big green waves; the houses on the quay were like dolls' houses; and high up inland, above the red cliffs and green fields, he could see the farm of Piggery Porcombe looking no bigger than a postage stamp. A little white patch in the orchard was Aunt Porcas's washing, spread out to bleach upon the grass. Near at hand the black tug "Sea-horse" smoked and plunged and rolled. They were winding in the tow rope which had just been cast loose from the "Pound of Candles".

Captain Barnabas stood up in the bows of his schooner; he yelled and shouted to the master of the tug. The sailors shouted also, and pulled with a will, and hoisted  the sails. The ship heeled over and rushed through the waves, and there was a smell of the sea.

As for Robinson—he tore round and round the deck like one distracted, shrieking very shrill and loud. Once or twice he slipped down; for the deck was extremely sideways; but still he ran and he ran. Gradually his squeals subsided into singing, but still he kept on running, and this is what he sang—

"Poor Pig Robinson Crusoe!
Oh, how in the world could they do so?
They have set him afloat, in a horrible boat,
Oh, poor Pig Robinson Crusoe!"

The sailors laughed until they cried; but when Robinson had sung that same verse about fifty times, and upset several sailors by rushing between their legs, they began to get angry. Even the ship's cook was no longer civil to Robinson. On the contrary, he was very rude indeed. He said that if Robinson did not leave off singing through his nose, he would make him into pork chops.

Then Robinson fainted, and fell flat upon the deck of the "Pound of Candles".

CHAPTER VII

IT must not be supposed for one moment that Robinson was ill-treated on board ship. Quite the contrary. He was even better fed and more petted on the "Pound of Candles" than he had been at Piggery Porcombe. So, after a few days' fretting for his kind old aunts (especially while he was seasick), Robinson became perfectly contented and happy. He found what is called his "sea legs"; and he scampered about the deck until the time when he became too fat and lazy to scamper.

The cook was never tired of boiling porridge for him. A whole sack full of meal and a sack of potatoes appeared to have been provided especially for his benefit and pleasure. He could eat as much as he pleased. It pleased him to eat a great deal and to lie on the warm boards of the deck. He got lazier and lazier as the ship sailed south into warmer weather. The mate made a pet of him; the crew gave him tit-bits. The cook rubbed his back and scratched his sides —his ribs could not be tickled, because he had laid so much fat on. The only persons who refused to treat him as a joke  were the yellow tom-cat and Captain Barnabas Butcher, who was of a sour disposition.

The attitude of the cat was perplexing to Robinson. Obviously it disapproved of the maize meal porridge business, and it spoke mysteriously about the impropriety of greediness, and about the disastrous results of over-indulgence. But it did not explain what those results might be, and as the cat itself cared neither for yellow meal nor 'taties, Robinson thought that its warnings might arise from prejudice. It was not unfriendly. It was mournful and foreboding.

The cat itself was crossed in love. Its morose and gloomy outlook upon life was partly the result of separation from the owl. That sweet hen-bird, a snowy owl of Lapland, had sailed upon a northern whaler, bound for Greenland. Whereas the "Pound of Candles" was heading for the tropic seas.

Therefore the cat neglected its duties, and was upon the worst of terms with the cook. Instead of blacking boots and valeting the Captain, it spent days and nights in the rigging, serenading the moon. Between times it came down on deck, and remonstrated with Robinson.

It never told him plainly why he ought not to eat so much; but it referred frequently to a mysterious date (which Robinson could never remember)—the date of Captain Butcher's birthday, which he celebrated annually by an extra good dinner.

"That's what they are saving up apples for. The onions are done—sprouted with the heat. I heard Captain Barnabas tell the cook that onions were of no consequence as long as there were apples for sauce."

Robinson paid no attention. In fact, he and the cat were both on the side of the ship, watching a shoal of silvery fishes. The ship was completely becalmed. The cook strolled across the deck to see what the cat was looking at and exclaimed joyfully at sight of fresh fish. Presently half the crew were fishing. They baited their lines with bits of scarlet wool and bits of biscuit; and the boatswain had a successful catch on a line baited with a shiny button.

The worst of button fishing was that so many fish dropped off while being hauled on deck. Consequently Captain Butcher

allowed the crew to launch the jolly boat, which was let down from some iron contraption called "the davits" on to the glassy surface of the sea. Five sailors got into the boat; the cat jumped in also. They fished for hours. There was not a breath of wind.

In the absence of the cat, Robinson fell asleep peacefully upon the warm deck. Later he was disturbed by the voices of the mate and the cook, who had not gone fishing. The former was saying:

"I don't fancy loin of pork with sunstroke, Cooky. Stir him up; or else throw a piece of sail cloth over him. I was bred on a farm myself. Pigs should never be let sleep in a hot sun."

"As why?" inquired the cook.

"Sunstroke," replied the mate. "Likewise it scorches the skin; makes it peely like; spoils the look of the crackling."

At this point a rather heavy dirty piece of sail cloth was flung over Robinson, who struggled and kicked with sudden grunts.

"Did he hear you, Matey?" asked the cook in a lower voice.

"Don't know; don't matter; he can't get off the ship," replied the mate, lighting his pipe.

"Might upset his appetite; he's feeding beautiful," said the cook.

Presently the voice of Captain Barnabas Butcher was heard. He had come up on deck after a siesta below in his cabin.

"Proceed to the crow's nest on the main mast; observe the horizon through a telescope according to latitude and longitude. We ought to be amongst the archipelago by the chart and compass," said the voice of Captain Butcher.

It reached the ears of Robinson through the sail cloth in muffled tones, but peremptory: although it was not so received by the mate, who occasionally contradicted the Captain when no one else was listening.

"My corns are very painful," said the mate.

"Send the cat up," ordered Captain Barnabas briefly.

"The cat is out in the boat fishing."

"Fetch him in then," said Captain Barnabas, losing his temper. "He has not blacked my boots for a fortnight." He went below; that is, down a step-ladder into his cabin, where he proceeded to work out the latitude and longitude again, in search of the archipelago.

"It's to be hoped that he mends his temper before next Thursday, or he won't enjoy roast pork!" said the mate to the cook.

They strolled to the other end of the deck to see what fish had been caught; the boat was coming back.

As the weather was perfectly calm, it was left over night upon the glassy sea, tied below a port-hole (or ship's window) at the stern of the "Pound of Candles".

The cat was sent up the mast with a telescope; it remained there for some time. When it came down it reported quite untruthfully that there was nothing in sight. No particular watch or look-out was kept that night upon the "Pound of Candles" because the ocean was so calm. The cat was supposed to watch—if anybody did. All the rest of the ship's company played cards.

Not so the cat or Robinson. The cat had noticed a slight movement under the sail cloth. It found Robinson shivering with fright and in floods of tears. He had overheard the conversation about pork.

"I'm sure I have given you enough hints," said the cat to Robinson. "What do you suppose they were feeding you up for? Now don't start squealing, you little fool! It's as easy as snuff, if you will listen and stop crying. You can row, after a fashion." (Robinson had been out fishing occasionally and caught several crabs.) "Well, you have not far to go; I could see the top of the Bong tree on an island N.N.E., when I was up the mast. The straits of the archipelago are too shallow for the 'Pound of Candles', and I'll scuttle all the other boats. Come along, and do what I tell you!" said the cat.

The cat, actuated partly by unselfish friendship, and partly by a grudge against the cook and Captain Barnabas Butcher, assisted Robinson to collect a varied assortment of necessaries. Shoes, sealing-wax, a knife, an armchair, fishing tackle, a straw hat, a saw, fly papers, a potato pot, a telescope, a kettle, a compass, a hammer, a barrel of flour, another of meal, a keg of fresh water, a tumbler, a teapot, nails, a bucket, a screwdriver—

"That reminds me," said the cat, and what did it do but go round the deck with a gimlet and bore large holes in the three boats that remained on board the "Pound of Candles".

By this time there began to be ominous sounds below; those of the sailors who had had bad hands were beginning to be tired of carding. So the cat took a hasty farewell of Robinson, pushed him over the ship's side, and he slid down the rope into the boat. The cat unfastened the upper end of the rope and threw it after him. Then it ascended the rigging and pretended to sleep upon its watch.

Robinson stumbled somewhat in taking his seat at the oars. His legs were short for rowing. Captain Barnabas in the cabin suspended his deal, a card in his hand, listening (the cook took the opportunity to look under the card), then he went on slapping down the cards, which drowned the sound of oars upon the placid sea.

After another hand, two sailors left the cabin and went on deck. They noticed something having the appearance of a large black beetle in the distance. One of them said it was an enormous cockroach, swimming with its hind legs. The other said it was a dolphinium. They disputed, rather loudly. Captain Barnabas, who had had a hand with no trumps at all after the cook dealing—Captain Barnabas came on deck and said:

"Bring me my telescope."

The telescope had disappeared; likewise the shoes, the sealing-wax, the compass, the potato pot, the straw hat, the hammer, the nails, the bucket, the screwdriver, and the armchair.

"Take the jolly boat and see what it is," ordered Captain Butcher.

"All jolly fine, but suppose it is a dolphinium?" said the mate mutinously.

"Why, bless my life, the jolly boat is gone!" exclaimed a sailor.

"Take another boat, take all the three other boats; it's that pig and that cat!" roared the Captain.

"Nay, sir, the cat's up the rigging asleep."

"Bother the cat! Get the pig back! The apple sauce will be

wasted!" shrieked the cook, dancing about and brandishing a knife and fork.

The davits were swung out, the boats were let down with a swish and a splash, all the sailors tumbled in, and rowed frantically. And most of them were glad to row frantically back to the "Pound of Candles". For every boat leaked badly, thanks to the cat.

CHAPTER VIII

ROBINSON rowed away from the "Pound of Candles". He tugged steadily at the oars. They were heavy for him. The sun had set, but I understand that in the tropics—I have never been there—there is a phosphorescent light upon the sea. When Robinson lifted his oars, the sparkling water dripped from the blades like diamonds. And presently the moon began to rise above the horizon—rising like half a great silver plate. Robinson rested on his oars and gazed at the ship, motionless in the moonlight, on a sea without a ripple. It was at this moment he being a quarter of a mile away—that the two sailors came on deck, and thought his boat was a swimming beetle.

Robinson was too far away to see or hear the uproar on board the "Pound of Candles"; but he did presently perceive that three boats were starting in pursuit. Involuntarily he commenced to squeal, and rowed frantically. But before

he had time to exhaust himself by racing, the ship's boats turned back. Then Robinson remembered the cat's work with the gimlet, and he knew that the boats were leaking. For the rest of the night he rowed quietly, without haste. He was not inclined to sleep, and the air was pleasantly cool. Next day it was hot, but Robinson slept soundly under the sail cloth, which the cat had been careful to send with him, in case he wished to rig up a tent.

The ship receded from view—you know the sea is not really flat. First he could not see the hull, then he could not see the deck, then only part of the masts, then nothing at all.

Robinson had been steering his course by the ship. Having lost sight of this direction sign, he turned round to consult his compass—when bump, bump, the boat touched a sandbank. Fortunately it did not stick.

Robinson stood up in the boat, working one oar backwards, and gazing around. What should he see but the top of the Bong tree!

Half an hour's rowing brought him to the beach of a large and fertile island. He landed in the most approved manner in a convenient sheltered bay, where a stream of boiling water flowed down the silvery strand. The shore was covered with oysters. Acid drops and sweets grew upon the trees. Yams, which are a sort of sweet potato, abounded ready cooked.

The bread-fruit tree grew iced cakes and muffins, ready baked; so no pig need sigh for porridge. Overhead towered the Bong tree.

If you want a more detailed description of the island, you must read "Robinson Crusoe". The island of the Bong tree was very like Crusoe's, only without its drawbacks. I have never been there myself, so I rely upon the report of the Owl and the Pussy Cat, who visited it eighteen months later, and spent a delightful honeymoon there. They spoke enthusiastically about the climate—only it was a little too warm for the Owl.

Later on Robinson was visited by Stumpy and little dog Tipkins. They found him perfectly contented, and in the best of good health. He was not at all inclined to return to Stymouth. For anything I know he may be living there still upon the island. He grew fatter and fatter and more fatterer; and the ship's cook never found him.

THE END